# Hiccup Effect
*Fight for Light*

J.N. Newmaster

Carpenter's Son Publishing

Hiccup Effect: Fight for Light

©2014 J. N. Newmaster

All rights reserved. No part of this book may be reproduced or transmitted in any form or by any means, electronic or mechanical, including photocopying, recording or by any information storage and retrieval system, without permission in writing from the copyright owner.

Published by Carpenter's Son Publishing, Franklin, Tennessee

Published in association with Larry Carpenter of Christian Book Services, LLC
www.christianbookservices.com

Scripture is taken from the HOLY BIBLE, NEW INTERNATIONAL VERSION®. Copyright © 1973, 1978, 1984 Biblica. Used by permission of Zondervan. All rights reserved.

Cover and Interior Layout Design by Suzanne Lawing

Edited by Bob Irvin

Printed in the United States of America

978-1-940262-77-2

**Dedication**

*To: Jaleena Jubilee and Nivian Nahvell
May your hearts always shine the Light . . .*

CHAPTER ONE

# Lights Out

The rolling thunder approached William, who found it fascinating to watch. He was one to always go looking at a storm from the back porch instead of hunkering in the basement, as advised. "It is said that getting struck by lighting is as rare as 1 and 1,000,000 and for teens and younger it becomes a 1 to 7,000,000 ratio. The odds were in my favor, or does that just make me favorably odd? Thunder on any other day besides this particular Wednesday would seem arbitrary; but this being the third of June…well, that would make it an unforgettable event in my history."

It is often the commonality of daily routines that bring about such pivotal changes. His gaze met the sky as a flash of lightning struck his eyes. The electric current collided with his internal nervous system, stopping communication from brain to muscles as William collapsed to the dirt. The storm raged on, oblivious to the aching and quivering body of this youth lying motionless. Lightning and thunder continued to chase and flee from an unseen pursuer.

A world of thoughts invaded William's mind as he lay curled up like a child. "I must not be dead or these conversations in my head would have stopped.... Although I feel heavy as a boulder sunken into the ground and my eyes feel like fire ... surely, I am not dead." William fought the comfort to stay hugging the soil and found the strength to stand. His knees trembled as his muscles tensed and flexed; he was finding the rhythm in his chest to be at a bit quicker pace. Salty rain broke free from his barricaded lids, attempting to escape such constraint. William desperately wiped his leaking, tear-filled eyes. But it was to no avail; the burning remained. He now opened his eyes and found that all was dark.

William began to regret making this bet with his friends. The late-night humidity stuck to William's face as he lay in that tiny tent, all alone in Blue Hill Forest. Why was William so afraid? It was not like he had never seen a thunderstorm before. William tried to reposition his body in his little three-by-seven tent. With the attempt to calm his ever-increasing nerves, William tried to remember all those nights spent with his dad under the back porch as the summer evening storms rolled in. *Boom!* These now distant memories of long ago leave him, sending William back to his fear-filled reality of immense thunder shaking his wet, 124-pound body to the core. It is amazing that what once seemed so peaceful now brought such fear to this thirteen-year-old boy. William looked at his watch, realizing there were three more hours till daybreak.

## CHAPTER TWO

# Never the Same

When the dawn finally gave way to the sun's morning glow, the colors had vanished and he could only make out shadows of black and white. William spun in confusion as he frantically searched for color: red, blue, yellow, green—anything to bring back familiarity. Last night's storm kissed goodbye all colored appearances from William's eyes; he was left with only shades of gray. What once filled the eyes in colored display now filled the mind with only gray. This blindness in color had opened new insight to reflections of good and evil. Adam and Eve in the Garden of Eden had their vision exposed to the fear and dread of the Lord, from disobedience, by eating the forbidden fruit. William now had this glimpse of the knowledge of GOOD and EVIL.

A worn-out horn beeping a tone of high to low a struggling melody pulled William to look at the classic white and green painted pickup truck wobbling up the dirt road. William looked down next to the tent and saw a turtle upside down, struggling to find a way back to its feet. William lowered to his knees, viewing it from ground level and flipped the turtle right-side up again.

William could remember clearly that the bet was to spend the night alone in Blue Hill Forest until morning, *hopefully surviving* and then be picked up by Charles. Charles was the much more mature, older brother of his best friend, Hector. William, still in confusion from his colored vision vanishing, heard the engine turn off and the door open. Charles stood before him, casually dressed in a well-worn pair of tan shorts and sweat-stained T-shirt. He was not alone.

Above Charles' head was a hovering, six-foot-tall, brilliant white angel of light. The strength of the angel was greater than any man he had seen; the angel was cradling a sword with ease, one obviously built by a master craftsman. There were feathers flowing from his shoulders down past his heels. The angelic being's mouth was moving, sharing words, but the words were inaudible to William's capable ears. William had been standing motionless, mouth pooling with drool of shock, when a familiar voice entered his ears.

"Ahhww man, I popped my tire." It was Charles, kneeling down by the back left tire of the truck. The tire was definitely flat.

"What are you standing there like a zombie for, William? Help me get this tire off," Charles said.

William was freaked beyond comprehension. He remained standing there, next to his burgundy canvas home, which now looked a dull gray to William's un-able to see color eyes, wet from last night's storm. He gazed his eyes back up to the angel, who was still floating in mid-air. William blinked a few times, rubbed his brown eyes, and realized . . . *Thud!*

"Ouch!" William shouted as he reached for his knee.

"Give me a hand, will ya!" Charles called out.

"That hurt, man!" William whimpered back in pain.

"Oh, sorry bud. I was just tryin' ta get your attention. Need a Band-Aid?"

"You hit my knee cap," William mumbled. Surprised by the piece of earth that had bit into his body, William darted his eyes away from the strong, angelic figure to survey his knee.

William's feet unfroze. He cautiously watched the angel as he approached the truck to help with the tire—not that he would be much help with this job. He failed auto shop class in the first week, accidentally setting a car seat on fire trying to remove a cigarette lighter. Stink hung onto William like a sloth lingers in a tree, while his usually lively hair was matted to his ears. William crumpled down beside Charles, their shoulders brushing.

As things began to calm a bit for William, the angel's words were no longer inaudible, but rang out boldly in his mind, while unnoticed to any other ears that would be nearby. *"Do not be afraid . . . You have been given a glimpse of hearts: some drowning in darkness, others breathing the Light. All will be shown as it will be. Peace I leave you."* William moved away from contact with Charles, which broke the communication from the angel's lips.

William was still feeling a bit panicky when he looked down at his knee and was distracted by his wound, which was leaking!

"Why does my blood look black?"

## CHAPTER THREE

# There Are More

Charles looked up, with curiosity, at the wound William had received. "What are you talking about? Your blood is red. Did you not sleep last night, or what?" Charles asked. William stared at his knee, from which, now, a tiny black stream ran down his shin and onto his tattered, water-logged socks, staining the edge of his leather-like hiking boots. While all this took place, the glowing figure held firm above Charles—in silence. William could not take his eyes off of the hovering form of white. Charles kept pressing the questions to figure out why William was in this funk. "You get stung by any venomous snakes or eat any strange-looking mushrooms, by any chance?" Charles asked.

William managed to utter, in a monotone, "No; I got struck by lightning."

"Oh, sure . . . that explains it," Charles said, reminding himself that the stories William shared were often large lies. Charles thought that if William was anything like Hector, his little brother, he was far from sharing the truth.

"Do you believe in Angels?" William asked, with a serious tone in his voice. Without giving pause to fixing his tire, Charles said, "Sure do. And you know, if there are angels, there gotta be demons too." Until they got back into the truck, William said nothing further.

The truck groaned and coughed deeply as Charles turned the key. The sound of the rumbling truck reminded William of his grandfather's old truck, calming his nerves ever so slightly. Charles drove from the forest on a gravel road along the River Epsilon. William let his gaze drift to the window and become engulfed with the sights that zoomed past. He saw the brightness of the sun reflecting off the river's currant; William tried squeezing his eyes tightly and opening them up several times, hoping to see with color as before. Each time William was disappointed to find the trees outside the window still a blur of gray, black, and white. They drove what seemed to take days as the plain leaves of gray slowly faded into suburban gray life.

The truck came to a halt at a stop sign. Both boys found themselves leaning forward from the sudden stop. A familiar face strolled past in the crosswalk. It was old man Wiker, who lived next door to William. But something had changed. It seemed that his shadow was not following his steps but rather forming an umbrella above his head. Why in this moment did William find his hands clenched into fists and the hair on the back of his neck standing on edge?

The immense darkness lurking above Mr. Wiker was not a shadow at all—but an angel absent of light.

## CHAPTER FOUR

# Fighting Fools

"Watch out, Charles!" William shouted as he pointed at Mr. Wiker walking across the road.

"Yeah, thanks a lot. You should have told me that ten seconds ago so I didn't almost smash my nose in the window," Charles said, pushing away from the steering wheel.

"What was that darkness above old man Wiker's head?" William asked.

"What's that? Watermelon tea? OK. Sounds good to me!" Charles sarcastically remarked, ignoring William's question. Now viewing Mr. Wiker from the back window and then the passenger-side rearview mirror, William asked, "You mean you didn't see that . . . that . . . thing . . . floating above his head?"

"What *thing*?" Charles asked, in what seemed to William like a spooky voice.

Now mumbling, William said, "There was a dark . . .a dark angel, just floating above . . . right above old man Wiker."

Charles blinked slowly, turned his head toward William, and gave a half-second-long dull stare, then yelled, "Oh my gosh! I see one right there!" as he pointed just above William's head with the index finger of his left hand.

"Where?" William asked as he looked all around. "Where?"

Charles calmly stated, "Oh, wait. It's just you."

"It's not funny!" yelled William as Charles began to laugh. "I saw something above that man just like I saw something above you this morning!"

William now looked out the window and sank down in his seat as his mind began to race with thoughts: *Am I seeing things? Am I delusional? My eyes did burn a lot this morning. Why can I only see white and black?* His thoughts continued: *Were those angels that I saw? Why was one full of light and the other form only with darkness?* William's heart was racing, but his face seemed emotionless, calm. Charles reached over to pat William's shoulder as a voice entered William's ears.

## CHAPTER FIVE

# White Noise

"*Peace, insight to have, in time to give, for you to keep, for you to share.*" The bridge was built, connecting once more the voice of Charles' angel to William's shocked ears.

Charles reached his hand toward the dingy plastic knob of the radio, breaking the bridge of angelic conversations. William was paralyzed for the second time in an hour from an angel speaking to him. And then, to make William nearly wet his pants, Charles's light angel—beefy strong—peered in through the window and smiled, holding eye contact for several moments, as if to say, "Yes, I just spoke to you." The glowing light angel then lifted from William's view, as if to catch a ride on the roof of the truck.

The static fuzz on the radio made William jump in his seat. Charles turned the knob again, stopping on the classic rock station. Charles sat back and continued driving, left hand on top of the steering wheel, right hand resting on the stick shift. Charles started tapping his fingers and humming to the sweet rhythms of classic '80s rock. William knew the song but could not hear the words on the radio. The sound of fuzz and static drummed in his ears. A soft, soothing voice from underneath the static began orating: *"William . . . yes, William . . . I know your heart, your secrets, your capabilities . . . "* William's jaw hung open. The voice caused his skin to sweat and body to stiffen in fear. He looked out his window, hoping to not see anything swooping by to say hello.

William kept telling himself, *This isn't happening. You're just having a total freak-out from last night's storm.* "Stop it!" William then blurted out.

"Chill out, we're here," Charles said as he pulled into the parking lot of Epsilon Eatery, a small mom and pop bistro that overlooked the scenic river, Epsilon. Its patio setting could barely seat 15 people and the décor was odds and ends of shades of red. William never had eaten at this breakfast and lunch time only restaurant. He never really thought about going there, but then again he couldn't drive and he was not about to go here with his mom on a date. The waitress was sweet and delicate and greeted them on the patio setting area. The locals knew the Epilson Eatery's special secret: homemade sweet watermelon tea. And so the seats were always filled during those hot summer days.

William's heartbeat seemed abnormal as he stepped out of the truck, perhaps an arrhythmia—or just shear panic. And yet, his mind was relaxed and his arms felt strong. Well, as strong as any other thirteen-year-old boy at 8:14a.m. on a Saturday morning after a daring night spent in the middle of Blue Hill Forest. William grew up in a town of sixty thousand people. He had lived a typical life with a typical family in a typical neighborhood.

His thoughts at this moment, though, were filled with a nauseating fear, a fear he hoped remained inside—instead of decorating the sidewalk with chunky vomit art. He wished he had brought his journal so he could vent somehow to the nonjudgmental pages about this crazy phenomenon. But he had not brought his journal with him on this little camping voyage.

"Wait," William said to Charles as he ran back to the truck. "I'll be right back!"

"I'm going inside to get us a seat!" Charles yelled back, with William now halfway across the parking lot. In the truck, William quickly scrambled through his backpack, frustration building on his face. "I know it's in here," thought William. "Don't say I left it in the woods. Ah, here we go!" William said as he began to zip up his backpack. Now running toward the restaurant, William realized he had forgot his money. Once more, William was running back to the truck. "Idiot! Where is your mind?" William said to himself out loud, as he opened the truck a second time. William jogged through the open setting patio to the back tables where Charles sat waving him his location. William sat down across from Charles, panting from his little run.

William was so frustrated in thought and so annoyed at himself that his mind was only paying attention to sitting down. "I got you some water," Charles said to William, even though William was already slurping his drink through a straw. The waitress walked up slowly, "What can I get for you?" In a much too formal tone, going with the overly polite demeanor as opposed to country twang which was expected in this neck of the woods.

"We both want turkey sandwiches and chips…and milk," spoke Charles.

"But it's breakfast time," said the confused, petite women wearing a vintage apron, embellished with her initial of A.

"Hey, you want milk too, right?" Charles asked William. Looking up from his glass for the first time since arriving, William's body froze.

His eyes locked on the scene before him. The patrons of the restaurant sat casually, unaware of the battle of darkness and light that went on just above their heads. Each person had a presence above them, floating as their shadow, a presence resembling an angel. The glowing figure above the waitress was white in color and female in gender. William glanced down to her name tag. "Angie," it read. William then moved his eyes to her mouth, which was chomping away at a big glob of gum. Then he looked the whole room over.

"Hun . . . you gonna' be alright with that?" accidently slipping into her country twang, interrupting William's overwhelmed state.

Charles spoke on William's behalf, realizing it was getting more awkward by the second of William's dumb found silence. "Sorry…Angie, he is a bit sleep deprived, we'll just have those sandwiches.

The waitress folded her notepad, placed the pin in her overhair sprayed up-do, rolled her eyes, and was on her way to make the order.

Charles kicked William's shin under the table. "What is wrong with you?" William made a sour face as he reached for his shin and thought, *At least it was on the other leg. It would be lame to have two wounds on one leg.* He focused his attention on a couple in their thirties that sat diagonal from their table. The wife had a white female angel that was lovely and elegant in appearance. He could see the angel was wearing an arrow satchel bag across her back and holding a long bow in her hand, armed and aimed at the husband's black shadow angel. The hovering Darkness figure was like a man, strong in stature and flawless in appearance. The Dark Angel held in both hands a sword that could have been larger than William's arms, stretched from fingertip to fingertip. William remained silent, watching steadily as the battle was underway.

The sword swung high and the darkness became darker as

the blade crossed mere inches from the soft, glowing face of the Angel of Light. While Charles got up to wash his hands, William continued to watch this movie-like scene play out before him. The white angel grew brighter as she fired her arrow toward the heart of the darkness. The arrow was deflected by the Dark Angel's toned, muscled arm, tearing away a slice of the being's "skin." His arm bled black blood. The blood fell toward the floor but vanished before reaching his feet.

The angelic woman of light with blazing hair reset her weapon, arrow toward the heart. She released the bow. The Darkness responded quickly from the wound received and brought his sword from the ground, diagonally up, right at her abdomen, missing her skin but destroying her set arrow. The couple's conversation was growing more intense, their volume increasing. The human man now stood, pointing fingers at the wife; the wife bowed her head, tears down her cheeks. The Light Angel brought a swooping blow with her bow to the Angel of Darkness, and the evil being staggered back. The husband left the table, also staggering to get away.

"So, how was last night's rain?" Charles asked, trying to normalize William's shocked expression. But his words were lost on William, still engrossed in the images before him. William got up from the booth and looked around the room, his mouth wide open. William was amazed, truly amazed at these new sights. Every person in the room had some form of a light or dark angel above their heads. Some angels were fighting and some angels were just talking. Even the white angels were talking to the dark angels. William wondered what they were talking about, for he could not hear what any of them were saying. *Why were more not fighting? Why were some of the light or dark angels not defending each other in their fights?*

Some angels just sat still as other angels looked like they were fighting to the death! But where was Charles' angel? Did he leave it in the restroom? Was it mad at Charles? William thought, *If*

*I was Charles's angel, I would probably leave him too. Does he always throw rocks at people and kick them?*

A sweet aroma swept into William's nose from a beautiful girl to all but her own reflection. Although breath taking in her yellow dress, she always seemed to feel internally inadequate.

## CHAPTER SIX

# Someone Pretty

William sat down once more across from Charles as the waitress, with a light glow above her head, balanced, ever so sideways on a tray, their order. "Here ya' go, babe," Angie said as she placed their plates in front of them. "I'll be right back with your milks," she said, turning to leave.

"Let's bless this mess," Charles said, thinking maybe some prayer would snap this kid into shape. Mumbling, Charles prayed, "Dear God, thank you or this food. Thank you for protecting William in the forest. Help us today to serve you. Forgive us of our sins. We pray this in Jesus' name. Amen."

"Amen," responded William as he opened his eyes and saw only white stars in his vision, thinking he had closed his eyes a little too tightly.

"William," Charles asked, suddenly looking very serious,

"Do you believe in God?"

William pulled his chin into his neck; he had never been asked this so directly before. "Well, yeah . . . sure." Charles nodded his head.

"Do you think we are to fear God or love God?" Charles asked.

"Ummmm, not really sure, but fear is definitely a familiar emotion right now. I must have seen too many scary movies, or maybe these crazy thoughts have to do with that spicy sausage I ate last night, because I think I can see angels."

Charles nodded again. "That sounds not *too* out of the ordinary for God; he often used angels to share a message to the world. Did you know that Satan is a fallen angel?"

"What? I thought angels were supposed to be good and sing songs all the time." William sat with his arms crossed, a bit stubborn to believe the whole situation.

"It's true. Satan was in Heaven before creation and he was God's best singer—even complimented for his beauty. So, you have heard the statement 'pride before the fall?' Well, Satan, or Lucifer as he was named, got super proud and thought he was god. But he wasn't, of course, and God threw him to earth, with a third of the angels with him. Pretty crazy if you ask me! Not sure how God works most of the time, but I do know it's a perfect plan, and that is hope enough for me." William had never heard this perspective, and he never had thought of angels before, but today was a day of a lot of new; and he was set to find the reason for why he was shown this insight of soul's eternal home.

In the seat behind William sat a young girl with delicate brown wavy hair, accompanied by three other girls. The young girl's name was Penny, and she was a favored student from his class. They never talked much, but he always found himself in class starring at her, watching her hand holding a pencil as she wrote notes from the board. She flicked her hair over her shoulder and it now rested on William's neck. He turned and noticed the girl, this girl of such beauty and popularity. His cheeks blushed and his heart thumped. The girls' conversations were swallowed up when a new, majestic voice spoke to William, sending a burning-fire feeling inside his chest. The voice called from the figure of grace behind him.

"You're not good enough; but you could be with my help."

"Excuse me," William said as he turned around to the seat behind him, accidentally pulling the soft, wavy hair that was resting on his neck.

"Aawww," cried the girl in a short, grunted statement, grabbing her hair and holding it protectively. Their eyes met and William's heart sank. He had forgotten how innocent she appeared. "You talk me?" he mumbled out. She looked confused. "I mean, you were talking to me, right?"

"Ummm, no. I am afraid not," was her polite response. William had cast his view upward, catching sight of a dark figure suspended above her that was staring deep into his eyes. William jumped back toward the table from the staring contest with this creepy darkness, bumping into the edge of the table with an elbow. The two girls across the table chuckled at William.

*Funny bones must be for those that don't smack them*, William thought. Surprised and embarrassed, he remained turned toward his plate.

"Who is that?" Charles asked, eyebrows lifting and winking an eye.

"Shhhh," demanded William, his index finger across his lips, "I'll tell you later."

"Oh, come on, Willy-Billy, cutie pie," Charles said, his head resting on the tops of his hands, batting his eyelashes like a girl.

"Later!" whispered William. "I'm ready to go home."

"Sorry," Charles quickly responded, "No can do. Your parents are gone for the day, shopping for your birthday presents."

"I'm thirteen years old! I'm big enough to be alone at the

house for a couple of hours!" William was concerned that Penny had heard Charles' comment. "I mean, come on! I spent all of last night in the middle of Blue Hill Forest by myself," William said in a louder voice, hoping that a particular someone might hear how brave and courageous he was.

After all, what is bravery without a woman to be brave for? What is courage except that which makes a young lady's heart flutter?

"Bye, Penny!" William said, shyly, as he left the patio set table. Penny's rosy, embarrassed cheeks already were apparent as she waved to cover her mouthful of waffle. "Bye, Penny," Charles said too, this time in a mocking manner.

Back in the truck, William looked straight up at the truck cab's roof and saw . . . nothing. He rolled the window down and adjusted the side mirror to see above the truck a pair of eyes staring back at him.

## CHAPTER SEVEN

# Friends or Foes?

The truck bumped up the curb to the house Charles called home. Waiting in the driveway was Charles' younger brother, Hector. Hector was putting off his most cheesy smile and waving his arm like an overcooked noodle.

"Get out of the way, you goof," Charles said, brushing his hand to the side as if it would push his little brother out of the way. William looked toward Hector, who was surrounded by five shadows of strong, dark, angelic beings. William's eyes opened wide, causing his pupils to enlarge, as if stepping into a dark cave. These faces showed longing and eagerness, like dogs on chains, constrained by an unseen leash, reaching out their arms at Hector. William watched the dark shadows staring at him as they smiled and nodded their heads in agreement to words spoken, but unheard by William. It struck him odd that their stares were not on his eyes but on something past him. William made an arched pattern with his head, looking from Hector to the truck. The early morning sun was bright, forcing William to reach his hand to block the sun's rays. William looked up again as he saw a man cloaked in strength and covered in darkness, standing a breath way.

"Hello, William," the guardian of darkness said. William's knees buckled and his body collapsed under itself; he dropped his backpack and collided with the grass—his head missing the concrete by a nickel, although he had been thinking of Penny before the black out.

William lay there, motionless for several seconds, but it felt like hours. William's eyes opened slowly and he rubbed the wetness from his face.

"Sorry about that," Charles said, holding an empty water bottle. "I always wanted to bring someone back by putting that weird-smelling stuff under someone's nose, like they use in movies, but I only had water."

"Am I dead?" William asked as he sat up, woozy from his fall.

"Yeah man, you're on the other side . . . walking toward the light. . . . Ooooohhh," Hector said, trying his best to sound eerie.

"Nearly cracked your head open, is more like it," Charles added. "You really took a fall."

"The woods must have made you loopy," Hector said. Hector moved closer to check his best bud, touching William's leg in the process. William could hear the voice of the Dark Angel, laughing from above Hector.

"That is right, stay on the ground! You can't get up, you're too weak." The voice was bold and the figure directed a thin, boney finger toward him.

Now it was Charles' turn to speak: "You gonna' be alright?" The five shadows were now making biting motions towards Charles's angel: taunting, throwing rocks, spitting, and the last one smiling. With fear and anxiousness in his voice, William tried to find the words to go on with this wild experience of a story.

"I have to tell you guys something." William felt alone . . . a painful silence filled his mind. Fear, mixed with numbness, now set in his self-aware dark heart from seeing his guardian being that of darkness rather than light. He wanted to cry, but he couldn't find the tears!

"God is real," William finally said.

Without a moment passing, Charles casually said, "OK, but even the demons believe God exists, and yet they shudder."

"What?!" said Hector, "What are you guys talking about? What? Did I miss something here?"

William felt nothing but silence as he sat next to the sidewalk that Saturday morning. What did those words mean anyway? "Even the demons believe God exists, and yet they shudder"?

This fear that William had was now turning into mental torture. William thought: *if the demons believe that God exists and the angels also believe that this same God exists, then what is the difference between the light angels and the dark angels?* Now William found himself starring at the five dark angels and the one white angel and thought: *what makes them different? Who is their God?*

At that moment, Hector and Charles' mom came running out the front door with two duffle bags in her hands, yelling as she ran toward the van. "The soccer game! We're late! Hector, come on! William! I've got your uniforms! You'll have to change in the van!"

William realized that he was running with Hector and his guardian of doom; but his gang of dark angels that had been taunting him was gone.

## CHAPTER EIGHT

# The Game

Distracting moments like these can change a person's focus by large measures—from extraordinary back to the ordinary. William lost his deep, soul-provoking thoughts of good and evil as he fumbled to remove khaki shorts for grass-stained ones. He grappled with how to tie his cleats in a way that would not easily untie, rather than what a dark angel was doing hanging out over his head. Both Hector and William were now fully engaged with getting their uniforms on. William looked up from attaching a shin guard and saw Hector deep in the pursuit of proper sock placement. William burst out laughing at the sight of his friend's appearance. "Maybe you should put your shirt on the right way, or are you trying out a new fad?" William chuckled again.

"Oh man!" Hector said, flinging his hands in the air.

This was the first moment William had been able to relax, even though only for a moment, since he had awoken this morning in Blue Hill Forest. Hector's mom brought orange slices and water along, which the boys snarfed at like tiger sharks on tuna, dirtying their jerseys even more and making their hands sticky. Their team, the Purple Hawks, was already warming up. The van door opened from the push of a button. Hector pulled on the back of William's collar, ungluing his face from the window and sending him crashing to the carpeted van floor. The contact with Hector's hand was only brief, but it brought a chilled from voice from the lips of a sinister form behind him that made William's stomach ache: *"You asked what makes us different? Come close and see my god."*

William chased after Hector to reach their teammates, who were now doing windmill stretches. Shaking his head to clear the creepy voice from his focus, William stumbled into the group.

Coach Hibky was on the outside of the circle, holding the roster on a clipboard. Without lifting his hat or his eyes, he said, "You're late."

"Sorry coach," said Hector, already out of breath. The coach began his pep speech, the one he gave before every game: "Today, we will be against one of the toughest defenses, the most aggressive offensive teams, the reigning champs, the Thunder Cats." The team was still stretching as he went on. "We, the Purple Hawks, have something they don't . . . we have heart. We have courage. We have teamwork. Determination! We wear our colors proudly. Why? *Because we're the Hawks! Are you with me, team?"*

Pathetically, only half the team gave a weak, collective "Yeah!" One enthusiastic "YEAH!" was called out by Aaron, the kid who had major social issues and tried befriending the coach way too much. The coach continued, a little disappointed in his team's lack of support. *"Are you with me, Hawks!?"* With real energy now, the team called back "Yeah!" as they threw their fists in the air. To everyone's amusement except their own, William and Hector were the two worst players on the team.

This was, after all, the reason they had become best friends. The last four games, William and Hector had brought a portable space heater and placed it under the benches, trying to have fun with the thought of being "benchwarmers."

"This stinks, man," said Hector as he sat there next to William on the eight-foot-long metal bench.

"You're telling me," William said, "My mom gives me this annoying 'I'm proud of you' speech before every game, as if I'm actually going to play or something. . . . Hey, did you bring any sunscreen this time?"

"Nope."

"What?" said William? "We're going to be sitting here for two hours, man. Last time, the whole left side of my face got burnt red!"

"Sounds like a personal problem," Hector answered, a small grin on his face.

"Hey," Hector continued, "what was that all about back there with the whole 'believing that God exists' thing? Are you turning all spiritual on me?"

With a loud, disturbing, and surprising burst, the voice of Coach Hibky thundered through: *"Hector! William! You're up!"*

With puzzled faces, William and Hector looked at each other and sprang up from their metal bench toward the field. Unaware that nerdy Aaron had tied their shoe laces together, the two fell like soggy socks. Hector and William kissed the grass turf with their hands up in the air, faces leading the way. Aaron, on the sidelines, fell backward, laughing. The two thirteen-year-old boys, who often got confused for being the other boy by their mothers, trotted to the field. Coach yelled once more at Hector and William, and then at Aaron, for the delay in joining the team on the field and for the shoelace nonsense.

After all the effort of straightening out their laces, the referee gave each of them a warning for improperly using the sidelines, and sent them back to the bench. Ten minutes later, the coach gave them their second attempt at "fame."

"Hey! You two!" Coach Hibky yelled. "You're up!" Once more, the two boys looked at each other, then down at their properly tied shoes before running onto the freshly mowed soccer field, already feeling victorious.

The whistle blew and the game continued. Both Hector and William positioned themselves close to the sidelines in hopes of avoiding any serious competition. To no avail, the coach noticed their scheme. Hibky yelled, hand cupped to his lips: *"Go get the ball!"*

Hector and William took off toward the ball like fruit flies on bananas. But the other team quickly maneuvered the ball away from the uncoordinated boys. The Thunder Cats passed the ball from player to player down toward the goalie. Hector was struggling to keep up with the ball. William was not even trying to get the ball, but simply lightly jogging down the field. The biggest kid on the Thunder Cats fired the ball hard with his right leg. He had aimed a little too high and the ball bounced off the goalpost and landed in front of William. William, stunned and nervous, starred down at his feet with hesitation.

"*RUN* William!" Hibky hollered. *"Go William!"* called Hector's mom.

William turned around, the ball now on his feet, and began kicking it down the field. *What is going on? Did that kid's angel just throw ninja stars at my angel? I don't know how to pass or score. When have I ever passed or scored?* William thought as he dribbled. He was midfield now as he faced an open field of green . . . Well; it was empty—other than the dozen kids and their evil or bright angels hovering around. With eyes narrowed, focused on the goal, he ran with all his might. *This is awesome! I won't be a benchwarmer anymore!*

But William's thoughts were interrupted as his heel began lifting from his cleat at the expense of a bullying Thunder Cat's having pulled the old "flat tire" trick. William only had time to look back and see the grinning face of the kid's aggression before smashing into the grass, left cheek down, feeling like it should be icing on a cake rather than dirt and turf. The cheers were turned to boos of disappointment. William remained on the ground, shoeless and annoyed. His pride came before his fall, he guessed.

Hector, being a good friend, came over and helped his buddy find his footing and his shoe. The whistle blew again as the referee announced a goal for the other team; his raised-arm signal revealed sweaty armpits. "Bummer," William said.

The game finished at: Thunder Cats 19, Purple Hawks 2. Hector and William walked off the field and to the bench.

"That was awesome!" Hector said with much excitement in his voice. "Dude, you had the ball for like ten minutes."

"It was like two minutes... OK five," said William, a smile now growing on his face.

"Yeah! You were like: kick, kick, spin, run, kick, kick," Hector said, a horrible mimic of William's foot movements.

"Yeah, I know; and then there was a *SPLAT*," added William.

"Splat?" Hector replied, laughing. "I don't remember a splat!"

Flashbacks of the game came back to William. These flashbacks were not of William's moment of fame with the ball, nor of his great fall for all to see. These flashbacks were now of a different sort—of angels and demonic beings dancing in what seemed to be a careful and care free battle cry. Kids on both sides of the field were just as aggressive as any other, despite their white angels or dark angels above them.

"How can I know?" William asked out loud as he was getting back into the van.

"Know what?" asked Hector, moving William's camping clothes off of his seat.

"Nothing," William said in a tired voice, trying to buckle his seat with the buckle backward.

Hector reached across the van and grabbed the seat buckle from William's hand, Hector's hand touching his hip in the buckling process. And then a statement that sent goose bumps up William's arms. With the coldest of stares, the most monotone of voices, and eyes looking straight into William, Hector's dark angel softly said, *"Maybe you should ask me for answers unknown, be more like me and love me. I will show you how to know."*

Ignorant of William's ability to see these angels in their splendor and the demons with their terror, Hector clipped on William's seat buckle and pushed the lever to close the door. William sat upright in his chair, halfway glancing at Hector, the other half looking forward.

The van lunged forward and sent the full cup of tea to the floor. Hector's mom had slammed on the brakes and stopped just in time, so the particular someone would not be flattened.

## CHAPTER NINE

# True Heart

"Aaron!" she called out in a frustrated tone, throwing one hand up. "That boy!"

Aaron waved back at the van that had nearly broken his legs, smiling like he had never smiled before. Aaron picked the ball up and trotted clumsily out of the way of the van. Both boys looked out of the front window, turned toward each other, and smiled.

"That kid is so weird," Hector said, shaking his head. "This one time, I heard that Aaron was trying to talk to Penny at recess and he tripped and landed on his face. When he got up, his pants tore open, exposing his little turtle undies. He ran inside crying while trying to cover up the massive rip with his hands. What a wimp." Hector laughed at the thought of it.

"Yeah, didn't you let him borrow those for the day?" William chimed in.

"Now Hector, that's enough. No more gossiping." Hector's mom spoke with discipline in her voice. Both boys snickered at being caught, but did not care.

The van continued on its way, the wheels rolling with a faint sound of gravel from the tires. The van pulled into William's neighborhood a little past five o'clock. The van teetered up the curb one wheel at a time, sending everyone's heads bobbing side to side.

"Hector, why don't you help William get his stuff inside?"

Hector grabbed William's backpack and said, "You're carrying your own smelly shoes."

"Yeah. Yeah." William tied the shoelaces and flopped the pair over his shoulder in fatigue. At the front door, William lifted his hand to give a high five as Hector responded with a palm down. Their hands hit and then slid away, reaching for their pockets, where they pulled out a finger gun, which they each used to mimic and chime in with an explosion sound. They blew the imaginary smoke away.

"See ya, man," Hector said as he walked away.

William waved bye and turned the dark metal doorknob and walked inside the cozy, lit home. "Helloooo. I'm home," his voice rang out. He could hear his mom working in the kitchen. He threw down his bags and walked down the hall, past the wooden staircase, and through the doorway into the kitchen. He came in smiling at the smell of cookies. He let his eyelids close as his nose pulled in every vapor of flour, sugar, egg, and chocolate possible. To his surprise, he kept his eyes closed a little too long and stubbed his toe on the corner of the doorway. He stumbled the rest of the way into the kitchen. "Are you alright, dear?" his mom said with concern in her voice.

William, no longer distracted by sweet-smelling aromas, realized for the first time the heart of his mother in its truest form.

## CHAPTER TEN

# Touch

What does unconditional love look like? If you could see unconditional love, what would your response be? Who could stand before this type of love and not be, at the least, at the bare minimum, overjoyed? You would hope that this fragile thing called life would allow you to—at least once—experience, maybe even touch, a real-life expression of pure love. Even if you had never seen this form of love before, wouldn't you at least feel . . . something . . . good? How does a person know, or *who* does a person have to know, in order to understand fully, without a doubt, that what they are experiencing is *real love*? What does it take? Or better yet, what does love require of that person in order to know that what they really see . . . is real love?

William, with all of his heart, thought he just experienced, for the first time, what he believed was the purest form of love, for he had seen his mother's angel in glowing light. It was the light of the angel representing the light in her heart. The most beautiful of angels he had seen among all the angels he had seen in less than 24 hours. William wondered what type of angel would be above his mother's head. Oh, how he had hoped it was a white angel. William thought he knew love. He thought that by seeing this form of unconditional love in an angelic being above his mother, that this would bring for him the same beautiful love too.

William's very soul began to battle within him as his mother's gentle arms wrapped around his shoulders and back, embracing him in a welcoming hug. William's mother's angel voiced to him a song sweet and melodious. *"Grace and peace to soon guide your ways, questions to seek and light to be seen."* The words seemed to release from the warm hug and the voice ended.

"I said I made some cookies. Would you like some?" she said.

"Cookies? Sure, I'll take some." Now eating a fresh batch of cookies, William thought to himself: "I knew it. I knew my mom was good."

"How about you come take a seat and tell me about your adventures in the woods and of the soccer game?" William's mom gently motioned toward the stool by the counter. William walked calmly; he had an eagerness to share.

"OK, so, sleeping in a tent alone during a thunderstorm was super cool," William said, speaking very fast.

"Weren't you scared?" his mother asked.

"Nah, I wasn't scared at all," William said, perhaps a bit overly confident. He then continued with his story, "I slept like a log or a rock, or something that doesn't move. While I was sleeping, a wolf came up to my tent and started scratching at my tent. It was growling and sniffing around the campsite, so I grabbed my pocket knife and flashlight and threw my door open. Well, I zipped it open really fast and yelled, 'What are you?' Then I realized it was a mouse digging at the marshmallow crusted to the tent.

"Then . . . I got struck by lightning. Thought I died. Now I can only see in black and white . . . and then I got breakfast with Charles and, well . . . that sums it up in a turtle shell or nut shell or something."

William finished his story with dramatic intonation, and halfway demonstrated the yell to his mom, making her jump.

"Wow, William. That sounds quite eventful. I am glad you were safe in the Blue Hill Campground." His mother obviously was thinking his son was playing the imagination card regarding the report of the lightning strike.

"Mommmm: Blue Hill *FOREST!*" William said, correcting his mother's failure to understand how childish it sounded as "campground" and how masculine it sounded when called a forest.

William's mom pulled her index finger to her lips. "Oh; I mean, Blue Hill *Forest.*"

But now William sat quietly, gazing at his mother's angel: white, brilliant, pure, lovely. He could not begin to describe the magnitude of its glow. The angel did not once take its eyes off of William's dark angel. The lips of his mother's white angel were moving, but William could not hear the words. He had heard other angels speaking before, but why couldn't he hear his mom's angel? William flashed back to all the situations in which an angel had spoken to him.

*That's it,* William thought. *We were in contact!*

William got up off his seat and casually walked to the counter, near the sink in which his mom was now working. He took his hand and placed it on his mom's shoulder. Instantaneously, William heard the voice of doves speaking calmly, but it was actually the voice directed from one angel to another. Trying to keep the situation appearing normal, William kept his gaze on the counter, but all the while he was listening carefully to the words being shared above him and his mother's heads. The bright angel spoke confidently to the darkness that floated above William's.

*"Light will be for all to see, darkness runs and melts away. No power in gloom when light is in the room."* William continued speaking with his mom while this battle of words continued. "It smells good, Mom. What are you making?" William asked as he inhaled, strongly.

"Oh, I am making lasagna," she said. William kept his hand on her shoulder. His dark angel spoke in a persuasive tone to the white angel. *"Light and darkness could not be without each other, you see. We are not different at all. Like the day and the night, each working together to create a full day."* Now the white angel interjected William's deep gloom that clung to his shoulder. The flowing angel of light swept the air and nearly brushed William's eyebrows. A raised sword, dazzled in precious stones, spun gracefully, hilt down to attack the darkness before her.

*"No, you false light deceiver! We are as separate as the east is from the west. Unless you do away with darkness and seek light fully, we will never be the same. Although you try to cover yourself in deception, your actions are still evil and the darkness remains."*

William pulled his hand quickly away in fear, stopping the forceful debate. "Well, I am going to take a shower now," William said, slowly walking backward away from the battle.

"OK dear, but don't be too long. Dinner will be ready in twenty minutes," she said while still preparing the salad.

William turned and ran upstairs. He went to the sink in the bathroom, placed both hands on the little porcelain sink base, and leaned his weight forward. He starred into the mirror and the angel above him was smiling back, wearing black armor held by thick buckles protecting his entire body, covering all with darkness except its face. William turned the water on and vigorously dipped his face into the water, washing his face intensely.

William looked up into the mirror at the dark angel that remained, and then whispered quietly: "Go away."

## CHAPTER ELEVEN

# Soap

William began to hear classical music playing from downstairs. *Dad's home!* He thought. Grabbing a towel, William began to dry off his face as he started to run out of the bathroom and toward the stairs.

"Hey William," yelled his dad from the downstairs living room, "Hurry up with your shower so I can take one next." William glanced quickly over his entire body and noticed all of the dirt, grass stains, and even the dried-up blood on his leg.

"OK!" William yelled back as he continued toward the stairs. *What is his angel like?* William curiously thought, *It's gotta be light. The whitest of white. It probably even glows brighter than mom's.* William crept halfway down the stairs and tried to catch a glimpse of his dad's angel.

"Did you hear your dad?" called William's mother, snapping

around the corner with a dish towel in her hand. "Now hurry up and take your shower." William jumped to his feet and quickly ran back toward the bathroom, turned on the water, and almost jumped in with his clothes on.

The music coming from downstairs became a faint sound of comfort to his ears. Now in the shower, William began to scramble for the shampoo and then the conditioner. What thirteen-year-old-boy uses conditioner but William? What thirteen-year-old boy rushes into the shower and still makes time to condition his short hair?

*Knock! Knock! Knock!* "Are you about done in there?" asked William's dad, standing behind the door.

"Yeah, about done! Give me two more minutes, Dad!" William yelled while dealing with a head full of suds.

"Are you using conditioner again, William?" asked his dad.

"Dad! Come on! I like the smell! And it makes my hair feel really smooth-like!" William yelled back.

"Oh, that's so sweet," teased his dad. "Now hurry up or I'll start flushing all the toilets in the house!"

"No!" William said, now laughing as he washed his entire body in about ten more seconds, dried off in but five seconds, and then ran down the hall toward his room with an over-sized towel wrapped around his entire body, from armpits to toes.

"Did you get your dirty clothes out of the bathroom?" asked William's dad from inside his own bedroom. Turning around in the hallway, William ran back to the bathroom, grabbed his dirty soccer uniform, ran down the stairs, and then to the laundry room, depositing his messy uniform.

The music grew and faded throughout the house as William turned each corner, hoping to see his dad's angel. When he heard his dad close the other bathroom door and turn on the shower, William grabbed his towel, lifting it above his knees, and ran barefoot back up the stairs as quickly as possible. Although his goal was to sprint up the stairs, he looked more like a dainty little girl running with a dress on. He had missed seeing his dad once again. William made his way into the room, sweeping some videogame magazines out of the doorway and under his dresser.

The dark angel lowered to the ground, wings, ink black, dragging behind him, leaned into William and said, *"Dream a world full of success, no trips or falls, no need for embarrassment or shame, all you do is play my game."* William was feeling vulnerable at this presence being so close and internally cold, yet radiating like fire. Although everything inside compelled him to be silent, he found a knot tugging at his chest, urging him to speak.

"Get back, Satan!" He was not sure where he had heard it, but it did the trick, and the angel vanished from sight.

William often heard his grandmother speak of guardian angels; what he never heard about was being guarded by a demon. No dust and no clutter that is visible to the eye were allowed in William's room. The pillow shape, visible under the forest green comforter, firmly tucked under on all sides, as if at a store on display. William acted annoyed at Hector's comments about his bunk bed; but actually, he really liked being able to sleep on the bottom bed one week and the top bunk the next. He had little items on the shelves next to his window; he displayed a few books that he was going to read this summer, but had not started to read yet. William walked to his bi-fold closet door. The door held a mirror, but only he stood in the reflection. It was nice, for once, being alone.

He pulled hard on the stuck knob, nearly sending him off his feet and losing the towel wrapped around him. But he regained his footing, and did not streak in his room. Shoeboxes, figurines, clothes, stuff of all kinds crowded the tiny, crammed closet. It was so cluttered and crowded that William barely managed to push away the mess and find a pair of red (although it may have been blue) basketball shorts and a fresh pair of boxers. He smelled them to make sure they were suitable for him to wear. He turned toward the entrance of the chaotic mess and dog-buried all his things between his legs, back into the closet.

He closed the doors as his toe pushed a jump rope handle back into the darkness. William sighed; disappointed at the mess that was his room. The bedroom did not represent him well, and he knew if it did not look clean, he would not receive his ten dollars from his parents at the end of each week. He walked to the dresser drawers, shirts thrown in randomly, and picked up the first shirt he touched. It also was red or blue. He held it up to his chest, not realizing the mistake of doubling on the red; it just looked dark gray to him. "Ahhhh," he sighed again, throwing the shirt back where he found it, and picking up a plain white shirt, wrinkled but clean; in this one, he could strongly see white, but colors were a bit tricky to determine. He took both hands and ran his fingers through his hair. "Silky smooth," he spoke out loud.

William heard the squeak of the wooden staircase, fourth step from the top. He stopped admiring himself and opened the door just as his dad was descending the stairs.

## CHAPTER TWELVE

# Wolves in Sheep Clothing

William's eagerness got the best of him as he sped through the doorway, slipping on a loose magazine that had not made it under the dresser—and he toppled into a wall. William's dad turned around at the commotion. "Whoa there, slow down sonny. So how was your game today?" His dad smiled, holding out his hands as if to catch him. William was smiling with excitement at seeing his dad, but his smile quickly faded as a shadow of darkness followed behind the man William admired the most.

William slowly walked to the stairs. His throat became tight, preventing him from swallowing. His heart sank and a fist clenched. William's father used the railing and casually made his way to the kitchen. "Game was good," William finally answered his dad.

"That's nice," his dad said, not looking back. William continued staring at the dark angel until he got to the dinner table. William managed to sit down, even though he never stopped looking at his dad's dark angel. His angel was motioning for him to come. The clang of pots and pans awoke William from his gaze. He had to distract his thoughts from his dad's angel, so he focused on the lasagna before him.

"Wow, Honey. It really looks great," William's dad said, with an over eager voice to please his wife, but empty sadness shown in his eyes.

With hands by her chin, mom politely responded, "Thanks, dear."

Politely responding to this little act of hospitality. "Let's pray," William's dad said as he began to bow his head, close his eyes, and fold his hands. William glanced quickly toward his mom, sitting across the small table, her "prayer mode" already in place. "Dear God," started William's dad, "thank you for this food . . . For my wife who so loves. . . . For my family . . ."

*Why is his angel dark?* William thought. *Why does he appear so plastic now, fake…like he is living two different lives. Nice dad at the dinner table and grumpy belligerent dad in his man cave?*

"Help strengthen us with this meal and bless this family. Amen," William's dad finished.

"Amen," William's mom said, followed shortly by an Amen from William. "That was a lovely prayer," spoke William's mom, with much delight in her sincere voice.

"Thank you," William's dad responded.

*It makes sense now why is his angel dark?* Thought William now able to see truth in his current reality and struggling to make sense of how share. *My dad is a great pretender. Year I could see the sadness growing in his eyes, seeing the closeness lost between my parents, saying they sleep in separate beds because "He snores." When really it's the lack of communication of their real hearts condition.* Fear was holding firm to William as he pondered his own hearts condition.

*Why is my angel dark?* Thought William time and time again. *My parents are two happy people. They don't fight. They always laugh and go on dates. They don't drink, much. They are both responsible and loving. They go to church... well dad sometimes goes to church, when it's raining and he can't go golfing. Why is his angel . . . ?* William's thoughts were interrupted by a question.

"Did you?" asked William's dad. Startled by his dad's question, William shook his head to regain his focus.

"What?" asked William in a clueless tone?

"Did you?" his dad asked again. William realized that his dad had been trying to talk to him for the last thirty seconds, but William had been staring into space with his mind picking up more unanswered questions with each passing moment, it seemed. "Did you stay there all night?" Dad asked for the third time.

"Uh, yeah," William said with an unsure response, not knowing if he gave the right answer.

"Wow, you did?!" William's dad asked with a father-like excitement and pride toward his only child. "You must have been scared . . . No! You weren't scared; you were brave, brave like a lion!"

"Yeah," William said, trying to sound as if he was up with the conversation.

"So where did you sleep? Did you stay where I dropped you off?" his dad asked.

"Yeah, all the other spots were full," William replied, with the sound of exhaustion in his exhale.

"Tell us more about the wolf you heard?" William's mom asked.

William continued. "Well, so . . ." But with his mouth crowded by lasagna, it sounded more like "Mel's toe."

"Who's Mel?" his dad asked.

William swallowed heavily and shook his hand left and right

as he said, "Not "Mel's toe...." Well, so."

His father nodded as he directed his son to continue with the story. William took a deep breath, opened his mouth really wide, and held up his fork for emphasis to continue his great woods story. But then the sudden ring of the phone stole the attention of everyone. William, air pulled in for an exhale just as he was getting ready to share the climax of his trip, exhaled all at once and shouted: "I'll get it!"

CHAPTER THIRTEEN

# Hushed

Stumbling into the corner of the darkly stained oak table, William reached out to grab the old '90s square beige phone, although he starting to realize he could see color with every 112th blink or so. The phones still connected to the wall were always described as dinosaurs by he and Hector, but the phone remained outdated, and yet functional. "Hello," William spoke, out of breath as if he just came back from a long run.

No response on the other side. "Hello?" William spoke again; some annoyance in his voice as his eyebrows squinted, wondering who this mystery caller was.

"Hey, it's me." The familiar voice of Hector was coming through the phone line softly. "Are you OK? Why are you whispering?" William asked, in a slight whisper himself.

"I am running away. Can you meet me at 9p.m. at the bus

station?" Hector had a muffled voice.

William turned and glanced at his parents, who had frowns of disappointment splattered on their faces because of this dinner time distraction. He smiled and mouthed, "Just one minute." William took his free hand and covered the side of his mouth with the phone to muffle his voice from being overheard by a loving, but nosy, mom. "Yeah, I'll be there," William spoke in a short burst.

"Bring twenty dollars," Hector said, hanging up the phone.

William, in a not-so-quiet voice, stuttered in confusion, "What? What for?" But the phone buzzed repeatedly in William's ear, informing him the call had ended.

He placed the phone back on the wall next to the picture of a fox in a meadow. William turned and walked back to the table. "Who was that, dear?" his mother asked.

"Oh, just Hector," William said.

"Everything alright?" his mom asked.

"Oh yeah, he just wanted to see what I was up to tomorrow," William said in a bored voice.

"Well, I hope you told him you will be busy tomorrow, because we are going to Aunt Sue's for her birthday party—remember?" She shot William a *I can't believe you would forget* kind of face.

"Of course I didn't forget," William said with false excitement—knowing full well he had forgot.

Dinner came and went with not much in the way of deep thoughts being shared. William got up to leave the room and his dad reached out his hand to stop him, when passing, to give a thought or two. The words his dad shared, however, were drowned out by the strong, booming voice of the angel, cloaked in penetrating darkness beside him: *"My son of same fate to roam together not alone, a strength in numbers we condone to take flight with friends spoken with on the phone."* William gasped and pulled away.

"What is it, William? I didn't mean to startle you. It looks like you have seen a ghost or something. Just making sure you got enough to eat and all," his dad said, apologizing.

"No, no, it's fine. . . . I just got light headed, that's all. Stood up too fast, I guess." His mom watched the scene and could feel a coolness creeping up her toes as her son passed by. She did not see the dark angel looming over her husband or blackness stalking her son, but she felt a chill more than ever, as if something evil were lurking in her kitchen.

The door closed tightly behind William and he quickly jumped to the floor of his bunk bed, then army-crawled underneath the wooden frame. "Where is it?" he mumbled to himself with frustration. "Aha!" William triumphantly declared after a frantic, five-minute search under the bed. Once the clanking around came to a halt, he backed out from underneath his sleeping haven, and with him pulled a metal box with a lock on it. The lock did not do much good since William left the key in the box key hole. He figured he would end up losing the key if he tried to hide it somewhere else. He turned the skinny key and waited for the click. He reached inside and found his beat up, faded blue Velcro wallet that he used to keep pennies and dimes in as a child. It now contained two hundred twenty dollars and some change. William was proud of saving up his money, but he did not really know what he was saving it for. *Perhaps something big and important; maybe a ring for Penny someday,* he repeated to himself each time he added his allowance. He frowned as he pulled out a twenty-dollar bill. William slammed the box closed and wadded up his once freshly crisp bill into his front pocket.

"I can't believe I am doing this," William said out loud. Looking at his watch, William realized he had only fourteen minutes remaining until he was to meet Hector at the bus stop. William quickly tied his laces in a tight bow and climbed out his window, onto the roof, and down the side of the house, and then ran in the direction of the bus stop. *Man, this bites,* William thought as he held the right side of his rib cage from the cramp he was receiving from being out of shape.

"Hey! Will," Hector said as he poked around a tree.

"Ahhh!" William screamed, like a sissy girl. "You scared the bajeebers out of me, Hector!"

"Sounds like a personal problem," Hector said, plainly. "Come on; we don't have much time." he added. And as he walked away, he had a dark, stalking angel following behind.

"What do you mean?" William asked in confusion as he pointed to the bus stop sign. "The bus stops just right across the street."

"What? No man, come on," Hector said as he now began to run in the opposite direction of the bus stop. William stood in place, unwilling to move.

"What do you mean, Hector? I thought you were going to run away?"

"Come on, I'll tell you later," Hector said.

"NO! Tell me now," William said, raising his voice.

"Shhhh," Hector said, grabbing William's arm and pulling him into the shadows of the trees. Instantly, William was able to hear the voice of Hector's dark angel, screaming loudly.

*"Come with me. You shall see the delights of heart. We will never part. Keep me close and find answers full and clear."* William stood still for a brief moment to regain his thoughts and rid his mind of this sudden fear of reality. William stood still, waiting for explanations.

"Tell me! Tell me or I'll tell Charles that you're the one that sold all his baseball card collection to get highlights put in your hair!"

"OK! OK, fine. We're going to Penny's house," Hector finally admitted.

"What!" William said. "Penny! Like . . . *the* Penny. . . . Penny?"

"Ok, how many times are you going to say her name?" Hector said with a laugh.

"I can't go to her house, "William said.

"And why not?" Hector asked.

"Because I'm supposed to be sleeping." William answered, a bit lamely.

"OK. Fine. Go home and tuck yourself in your bed and start dreaming about me and Penny going on a date. She's wearing a purple umbrella dress, or something romantic like that, and I am wearing a white suit with green pinstripes. And while you're dreaming of our big-powerful-amazing date, make sure that you add in that big kiss that she's going to give me!" Hector continued: "Just imagine a big pair of lips the size of a watermelon, kissing . . ." William could envision this "date" and the image of Penny's lips growing to a massive size, getting ever closer, until finally landing on Hector's cheek. The image exploded in his mind and William fanned it away with his hands.

"OK. OK. OK. I'll go. . . . I'll go," William said.

"Why the sudden change of heart, William?" asked Hector, mischievously. "Is it 'cause you want Penny to kiss you? Huh? Do you kinda' think you'll marry her? Are you going to read her a poem of words expressing your love and affection for her?" Hector asked, using a girly voice imitation as William just stood there, half annoyed and the other half blushing with denial.

"Come on, let's go," William said as he started walking in the same direction that Hector had begun to run in earlier.

"Hey, did you bring the money?" Hector asked.

"Yeah," William said as he took the twenty dollars from his deep pocket.

"Thanks, man," Hector said, snatching it form William's hand.

"Why did you need it?" William asked.

"I don't. I just figured you would be gullible enough to give me some of your money," Hector said as he began running away from William, laughing loudly and yelling, "I'm rich! I'm rich!

I'm rich!"

"What?! Give me that back, Hector! Give me back my money," William said with a small smirk on his face as he ran down the street after Hector.

As the boys made their way unstealthily to the girl of William's dreams, William could feel all of his nerves tightening—or was that his belly churning?

## CHAPTER FOURTEEN

# Window View

Penny was sitting on her "beauty stool," facing her rounded mirror, brushing her hair. Penny brushed her hair like this every night, ten times on the left and ten times on the right—just as her mom had before she passed away two summers ago. Now it was just her dad, her pet gold fish she had won at the county fair, and a dog that was older than dirt, named Thud. Penny's room was situated close to the back patio, just a room away from the living room, where her dad was sleeping on the couch. A dark, heavy-set, thick-necked angel sharpened a knife above his host. A battle was not at hand, but the angel was preparing for one. The TV was still turned on, buzzing with commercials.

The boys quieted down as they approached Penny's house, at the corner of Mulberry and Pine. They had been by this house a hundred times, always too scared to knock on the door. Penny was the girl in school that all the boys crushed on and all the girls jealously wanted to be. Despite all of this, she remained quite ignorant of her admiring fan club, feeling hopelessly inadequate.

Now acting like a spy, Hector whispered and pointed. "Look. Look. Her light is on." William had trouble swallowing. He felt like his throat was full of sand, or a large shoe, or two tons of nervousness.

"What is your problem? She's just a girl," Hector said, trying to lighten the anxiety they both felt.

*Only the coolest, most popular, prettiest girl in all of Loveland,* William thought to himself, then blurted out loud: "I can't do this!"

"Shhh," Hector spoke, forcefully, covering William's mouth with his hand. "Come on, wimp," Hector said, dragging William by the arm. They could see that her window was open and the screen was down. They perched below the window, backs toward the wall, knees to their chests, breathing nervously. Hector began rising slowly up to the side of the window.

He peered in and could see Penny sitting on her stool, facing the mirror as she placed the brush on her dresser. A fan was placed across from the window, creating a breeze on the flowery blue curtains. Hector nearly fell over at the powerful, pleasant fragrance that drifted through. William steadied his friend and tugged his wrist to get him to sit down again.

"Well, what did you see?" William asked, eagerly. Hector just smiled with a grin bigger than his face. William snapped his fingers in front of his friend's face and whispered, "Come on! What did you see?" Hector remained still, unresponsive, and awkwardly cheesy-faced. William's new found bravery—more curiosity than bravery—compelled him to take a look for himself. William placed his hands on the sill of the window and peered over the ledge.

Penny had gotten up from her beauty station and was turn¬ing on her CD player, which sat next to her well-put-together bed. Her hair damp from a shower shined in the glow of the lamp above her. Her angel, armed for battle, could have passed as a Hawaiian beauty pageant winner if not for the crossbow slung over her back and evil stare in her deep, black eyes. The wings ruffled like a crow getting ready for flight. Penny, unaware of the elegant, creepy angel hovering over her head as a tainted halo, began to sway her arms to the rhythm of the music.

She was wearing her PJs: plaid pants with a matching button-up shirt that she received from her dad, who assumed his style was her style. Her dad did not understand that most girls prefer pink; not Penny particularly, but then again, she was not like most girls. William's jaw had dropped in the grace and beauty of this beautiful girl in blue cotton—or was it purple? William was realizing that if he could refrain from blinking as long as possible, the images would remain in color for longer moments in time!

*How could she have a dark angel?* William was so intrigued by Penny, her bold comments in class, her strong air of confidence on the playground—and all of that to cover up a girl who eagerly hoped for approval and affection. She felt never good enough.

The window was not well secured and creaked loudly from the weight of William's hands. Penny sharply turned and faced the window, surprising William, who fell straight onto his rump. Penny ran to the window and lifted the screen without hesitation. William sat frozen to the grass as Penny peered into the yard, her night vision impaired by the change from sudden indoor bright light to outdoor night lighting.

"William?" asked Penny. William did not know what to say. He stared at Penny, and then toward Hector, who was motioning silently for William to look at Penny, not him. "William, is that you?" Penny asked once more.

Hector, his eyes widest of all three of them, was mouthing the word "yes" toward William as he shook his head up and down. William, sitting on his rump, was smiling from ear to ear at Penny.

"Umm, yes . . . Hi, Penny," said William in a short burst, plenty cheesy-faced. William's eyes began to look past Penny to the angel haunting her shoulders. The angel was waving, her eyelashes blinking dramatically and giving him a wink. William did not like the idea of a spooky demon chick trying to flirt with him, especially in the presence of his true heart's delight.

He quickly looked down to the ground in search of something to say. His eyes widened and his posture straightened as his mouth began to speak. "Who would have thought that we would see each other twice today? It's kinda funny, right? Ha-ha," William forced out, quite lamely.

Hector shook his head furiously left to right while mouthing "NO! NO! Idiot!"

Penny responded with a half-smile: "Yeah, funny."

"I'm sorry, "William said as he quickly got up to his feet.

Penny took a couple steps back into her room to pause the music and then leaned forward once more and asked in a firm tone of voice: "What are you doing by my window?"

Hector began to act like he was kissing an invisible girl while miming the words: "Love, Love, Love, Penny, Penny, Penny." William's face tightened, hoping Hector would stop making so many distractions.

"I wanted to see you," William said, surprising himself with his own words.

"You did?" asked Penny, more curiosity in her voice than she expected. Hector sat up; stunned that William would be so forward.

"Yeah, I was thinking about you today, Penny, during my soccer game," William said, not knowing himself what he was going to say next.

"You did?" Penny asked.

"Yeah," responded William. "I . . . I wished I had said something to you at the restaurant earlier today."

"Really? What did you want to tell me?" asked Penny, now giving her full attention to William. She felt like a princess in a high tower about to be serenaded by a prince, or rather the class goof ball.

William's confidence seemed genuine, but inside his stomach was churning, literally churning. It was a loud enough rumble that Penny angled her head a bit, wondering where the strange sound was coming from. William lifted his hand as to give a grand speech, but when his hand stretched just above his brow, William farted—loud and long. William could have died from embarrassment... Penny covered her mouth in shock at such a romantic scene turned sour. William feet glued to the grass below and his hand raised to the sky, gave the most awkward of smiles to the love of his life.

Hector jumped up from under the window, grabbed William by the arm, and started running, hard, leaving puzzled Penny all alone at her window sill.

Hector was unable to keep running due to his hysterical laughter at his best friend's great display of affection. Now out of sight from Penny's house, Hector stopped.

"What was *that*?" Hector said, laughing strongly and holding his knees. William once again had fiery red cheeks.

"I blew it! Why did I have so much lasagna?" William said, hands on his head.

"Yeah! You blew it alright . . . with a fart bomb!" Hector said, unable to stop his laughing.

William looked at Hector and said, "Well, I'm going to go dig my grave . . . see ya, bud."

Hector nodded, still chuckling to himself. "See ya."

William hurriedly made his way back home, not realizing

how much the night had vanished while being in the presence of such a princess. He came up to his well-lit house and could see his dad in the living room, reading a big novel of who knows what. The figure above his dad did not seem all that forceful and appeared to be resting its back on an invisible wall. Its cloak was torn from a battle nearly won. William continued to his room, up the lattice, onto the roof, and through the window. William reached his room without any complication. He felt a wave of tiredness plowing into him and decided to skip his night time routine of brushing his teeth. Instead, he went to his bed and flopped down on top of the covers, too lazy to change into his PJs or to get under the blankets. He faced the wall, and then heard a creeping voice growing louder from above where he slept.

## CHAPTER FIFTEEN

# Faded Past

Eight hours went by with William tossing and turning on his sheets, struggling to make sense of his nightmare-reality; zero minutes of that wonderful REM sleep actually occurred. Not the *beep beep* of a clock, but the ever-so-exciting vacuum on the stairs trick that his mom liked to do is what woke him. *Couldn't she just come in the room and calmly say, "Time to get up, William?"* No . . . it was Sunday: house cleaning day. *Didn't Grandma Eugene call this day a day of rest?* William pondered if it would ever be true.

"Hurry," his mom called from a distant room, downstairs. William went on auto pilot as he got up and went to do his morning business and wash his face. He must have kicked off his shoes and socks because his toes were naked on the tiled bathroom floor. "William!" his mother called from the hall.

"We leave for your Aunt Sue's birthday party in fifteen minutes."

"OK, Mom!" William called back. "Greeeeaaat," he muttered under his breath.

William gazed at himself in the mirror. "You're still here." He said to the darkness that stood behind him, mimicking his hand motions through his hair.

*"A true sight to see: this bond between you and me, like a close-woven net to be a forever-lived debt,"* the angel said, flexing his biceps and gripping a small dagger in each hand. His angel was in need of an attitude adjustment and a face lift. The angel's cheeks seemed sunken in, as if at any moment he would be blowing out a candle. His neck pulsed as from heavy lifting and his throat dramatically swallowed, thirsty to encounter an angel of light. William began to notice a theme in the angels he had encountered the past two days: they seemed beautiful, strong, and ready for battle. What were they battling over? Souls? How would his actions affect the actions of an angel around him?

He was not sure, but he was going to find out.

Now in the van, William tried to collect all his thoughts. *I wonder what Penny is doing right now? Man I ruined it last night!* William's mind was analyzing every move, thinking what he could have done differently and wondering if Penny even had a single bit of interest in him.

Believe it or not, William had been quite successful with dating—if he actually understood the word. His first real girlfriend was in second grade. Rosie Swandel. What a lovely name. She was shy, smart, and funny . . . or, more oddly, unique. She had a great taste for clothes but always smelled her hands. It was kind of a weird thing. She carried around four or five different lotions, each with a unique smell, especially the one that smelled like Brussels sprouts. They must have been organic lotions or something. William and Rosie dated for 17 hours, sadly ended by a heart-breaking letter from Rosie's friend, Sharla. It read: "Dear Willworm, Rosie said your hands stink and that she can't date you anymore. – Sharla." Ouch.

The second girlfriend of William's was in the fifth grade. Her name was Shaerab Smalls. She was new in school and became the fresh hot stuff for all the fifth-grade guys. One day, Wil¬liam noticed three guys making fun of her name; calling her "show-ri-ra," "sha-ra-ra-de" . . . he guessed the "d" was silent. Others called her "Shady Rabi" and "Sha-rabies." William, who was trying to join in on the name-calling, gave his first try at it, and calling her "Sarah." Low and behold, he pronounced it right. He then guessed that the "b" was silent and the "h" too. Russian language was tricky to pronounce.

 Shaerab was a foreign exchange student and not shy at all, claiming William as her knight in shining armor for standing up to those big name-calling bullies. William never had the guts to tell her the truth. William and Shaereb dated five whole weeks! But they never really talked much: no phone calls or meeting up at the movies, no love letters. Not much of anything, really. One day William saw her walking toward her bus after school. He ran up to her and said, "Shaereb, I don't want to be your boyfriend any more. We don't talk much. All we really do is wave at each other in the hall." She turned to face him, politely responding with, "Umm, I never knew we were dating . . . but OK," then turned to get on the bus.

*Ohhh, that sucks! I am such a LOSER!* William voiced loudly in his mind and ran red-faced after his bus. OK, so maybe William really only dated one girl. *They both must have had really dark angels over them,* William now thought.

William stopped his painful memories of his failures at social skills and stared out the window, seeing Aunt Sue's house sitting against the crisply green manicured lawn. "Whelp, we're here," William's dad called out.

They walked up the curving cottage-like walkway, toward a magazine-like photo shopped red door. William's dad stepped up the concert step toward the door. His dad's angel swooped down to the welcome rug and bunched it up, causing his dad to stumble toward the door. The white angel above his mother pushed his mom's arms to steady his falling dad, before he nearly smashed his head into the doorknob. William's angel laughed from above at the near mishap, although both dark angels would have liked to see a worse outcome. William reached out to help regain his dad's footing. The dark angel above his dad turned to William, winked, and said with teeth bright and clean, although William expected them to be sharp like a sharks: *"A stumble is one step closer to a fall."*

## CHAPTER SIXTEEN

# Secret Swap

It had dawned on William that he did not have a gift for his aunt. Not a present, not a card, not anything for Aunt Sue's birthday party. William wasted no time as he quickly traveled down the hall, looking cautiously to his right and left, then looking back to see if anyone might be inside. Realizing he left the front door open, William ran back to close it. In the living room sat a table, piled high with gifts, wrapped eloquently and with much care. William noticed all the girly little bows affixed tightly to the many patterns on the wrapping paper of each precious gift.

He could feel a tightening in his chest as he thought of claiming one of those gifts and writing "From: William." Who was he kidding? He was no handyman, and he couldn't make her something from nothing. His angel's voice entered his thoughts.

"William, no one will see this small thing. Claim a gift for her from you; it would be better to have than to not; go on, quick, before someone comes."

He looked at his surroundings to check that the coast was clear, and then ran to the gift table. His chest hurt even more as William crept closer. He stopped to rub his heart. *Hmm, must have heartburn . . .* He continued with his sneaky plan as he ripped the card off of a present in the middle of the table. It looked like the size of a shoebox. Not the biggest, nor the smallest. He found a stack of note cards in a nearby drawer and wrote the words, "To my favorite Aunt, Love William." The back door opened, startling William, and he quickly placed the present on the table from which he had taken it. William calmly turned and casually began to stroll down the hall to gather with everyone outside. Turning a corner, he nearly collided with Aunt Sue.

"Oh, honey bunny cuddly cakes! My, my! How you have grown!" Aunt Sue spoke, a bit squeakishly, in a slightly bent down-to-his-eye-level kind of way. William felt a pinch in his chest again, this time from the guilt of almost getting caught by his Aunt Sue, along with the pinch of the chicks. *Why do they always do that?* Thought the bruising cheek William.

"Hi Aunt Sue. . . . Happy birthday to ya!" William said as he pulled his chin down in partial shame, but unwilling to admit it. She escorted him through double glass doors, holding him by the shoulders. His aunt's angel, glowing light, beamed a voice soft and gentle. *"Dearest one, you need not impress with false affections, your actions are her joy, be genuine and true to set your heart free from this guilt you bear."*

Upon seeing a straining look on William's brow, William's mother spoke a welcoming greeting, "There you are. We were beginning to think the cat ran off with you, ha ha ha." Stepping over to rescue William from the awkward embrace, she leaned in to whisper, "Everything all right, Will? I noticed you struggling to relax with Aunt Sue.

"I was just feeling a bit claustrophobic with all her kisses, not to mention the strong lavender-soap smell," William said, covering his nose from any more bad odors entering.

"You will get that when you turn older than 50; they go with strong perfume to hide their aging smell." Mom was being quite witty this afternoon.

They both chuckled in secret, standing by the red punch bowl with an ever-melting, floating sorbet chunk. The birthday party carried on in a sluggish fashion, meeting and greeting family and more, smelling of mothballs and lavender soap. Everyone talked and ate as William just sat in a daze, holding a plastic cup of punch, thinking back to the night that he camped in Blue Hill Forest.

*Am I really the only one who can see these angels in dark and light? Will I get struck by lightning again and lose this ability to see these things? Maybe I could get struck by lightning again and lose this terrible color-vision problem.*

"Isn't that right, William?" his mom asked. William, however, remained in a trance. "William?!" his mom called again.

"William!" This time his dad called to him in a louder, command-like voice, snapping his fingers in front of William's face to get his attention.

"Huh?" William asked, in confusion.

"Your mom's trying to talk to you," William's dad said.

"I'm sorry," William said as if he had just woken up, "What did you say, Mom?"

"It's OK," his mom said. "I was just telling your Aunt Sue how excited you are to go to camp this Wednesday."

"Oh, yeah—summer camp," William said plainly as he looked down toward his drink. "Hey Dad," William asked, looking up, "do I have to go to camp?"

"I thought you liked summer camp," his dad said to William.

"Well, I did. It's just that . . . I've gone every summer for the last three summers and I was thinking that I could stay home this summer, or something."

William's dad turned toward his son and replied, "Sure, William, if you want to stay home this summer, you can."

"Really?!" William asked, looking at his dad. "Really?" Now he was looking at his mom, who gave a smile as if to say, "Yes, William. Really, you can stay."

Last summer camp was the worst five days of William's life. His mind flashed back to a particular moment at camp: the second day, leaving to go to canteen, which was breakfast in the cabin at the center of camp. William could still recall the smells of warm maple syrup on fluffy waffles, filling his nose with the fragrance of liquid sugar. Feeling proud and confident, William walked to sit with a group of friends, until uproar of laughter broke out from behind him. William discovered the laughter was because of a melted chocolate bar purposefully placed at the back seam of his khaki shorts; this was a favorite hazing trick by the older boys of cabin four.

Another embarrassing moment entered William's mind: craft time. While building a miniature boat out of popsicle sticks, William's strength snapped the tiny wooden stick in his hands, sending a splinter into his eye, and leading to his falling off the bench with a double dose of bruised backside. Those around laughed once more at this complete display of professional clumsiness.

Another day at camp William tried to make a torch out of a few marshmallows on a stick. Once aflame, William swung the stick in the air to distinguish his burnt mallows. With uncoordinated maneuvering, he torched one of the counselor's hats. The counselor, however, did not find it very funny and placed William on potato peeling duty for the rest of camp.

William refocused his eyes to come back to reality and, with a shake of his head, discovered his parents gathering their things, for the party had come to an end. Yes! He thought to himself, punching and pulling his fist to his side. William began to think a little more on what to do with his light and dark ability: *Should I tell someone? Would it even help? What good would it do to be thought of as a crazy person? They would just lock me in a loony house.* William felt relieved by one thing, at least: not having to go to summer church camp at Happy Howard Ranch.

William's day was coming to an end as the sun faded into the pinkish-orange sky. When he and his parents arrived home, there was a man standing at the front door, facing the street, expressionless.

## CHAPTER SEVENTEEN

# Bad Company

"What is Mr. Wiker doing at this hour?" asked William's mom, with confusion in her voice.

William's dad stepped out of the van and spoke in a calm tone: "Hello, Mr. Wiker. What brings you to our door this evening?" No answer. No response. He remained frozen, standing at the door. Mr. Wiker always seemed odd and overly creepy. Wiker finally spoke up: "Lost my remote. Eeeeeh, I can't turn on the TV without the remote . . . Can I watch your TV for the next forty-five minutes or so?"

"Uh, sure... Sure thing," William's dad said.

"Much obliged," Mr. Wiker said.

They all walked inside, Wiker sat in the chair closest to the TV as William and his parents walked to the kitchen. In a whisper, William asked his parents: "What's he watching?"

"I don't know," his mom said. "Some old movie."

"Would you like something to drink?" William's dad asked Mr. Wiker.

"No, no thanks," Wiker answered. William walked into the living room and sat on the chair next to Mr. Wiker. The dark angel above the bent-backed neighbor seemed to have fallen asleep standing up. There was a knock on the front door. William jumped up from his chair and jogged to the door.

His dad yelled out, "William! Let me get the door." Just as his dad began to open the door, the doorbell rang. It was Hector.

"Oh, sorry. I didn't know you were at the door," Hector said to William's dad, who waved for Hector to come inside. William was leaning against the couch as he greeted Hector.

"Hey, Hector."

"Hi," Hector responded, staring at Mr. Wiker with a confused expression on his face. "Uhhh. Hi, Mr. Wiker," Hector said with difficulty, receiving no response. Five seconds later, Mr. Wiker turned toward Hector, nodded his head, and smiled at Hector, then turned his gaze back toward the TV.

"So, you want to go to my room?" William asked Hector.

"Sure," responded Hector, with a get-me-out-of-this-room kind of facial expression. "Do you have any soda, or something to drink?" Hector asked.

William shook his head no, adding: "And dinner is in one hour."

"Then I'll take water," Hector said. "Hey, could I stay for dinner? My mom and dad are at some meeting and Charles is in charge of dinner tonight. He doesn't even know how to flip a pancake."

"Let me ask my mom. Stay in my room," William said. William ran to the kitchen and called for his mom. "What are we having for dinner?"

"Candy and ice cream," she said with a straight face.

"What?" William said, caught off guard.

"Chicken noodle and stuff," she said.

"Can Hector stay for dinner tonight?" William asked his mom.

"No, I've alrea—"

"Oh, come on!" William interrupted.

"I said no," his mom calmly spoke. "Besides, I already invited Mr. Wiker to stay with us for dinner."

"What!" William said in a loud whisper. His mom shrugged her shoulders and continued on her way. William walked back to his room to deliver the bad news.

"Sorry, man," William said to Hector, handing him a plastic cup of water. "No, it's cool," Hector replied.

"My mom said she already invited Mr. Wiker for dinner," William added.

"What!? Mr. Wrinkle Worm!? You're trading me in for that old fart! I gave you the best years of my life and this is what I get in return?" Hector said with a grin on his face.

William burst into laughter and said, "Yeah, pretty bad, right?"

"Have fun eating next to that loon," Hector added, making fun of William's dinner date. "Do you think he's going to want to share forks with you or have you feed him?" Hector continued, which led to William laughing more. "I dare you to fart and blame it on him!" Hector said.

"What? Come on! No way!" William said, still laughing. But he added that he was quite terrified to share a table with the man downstairs.

Hector sat on William's bed and noticed a Bible on his bed stand. "You have a Bible?" William shook his head yes, but he also felt a bit unsure as to why he felt shame over this.

"Do you actually read it?" Hector asked, full of curiosity.

"A little. I mean, I just started reading it again yesterday," William said.

"So what book in the Bible are you reading?" Hector asked.

"So far, just the Pro-face."

"Pro-face?" Hector asked, now confused. "You mean *preface*," Hector said with a little laugh. "That's not part of the Bible. That's the introduction pages before the book!" Hector continued: "That's funny! So I guess God wrote the index and dictionary too?"

"OK, I get it," William said, with embarrassment in his voice. "I guess that explains why none of it made any sense." William kept his composure despite the awkwardness he felt at being embarrassed by his best friend. Although Hector laughed at William's bit of ignorance, he held a respectful interest and even a sense of curiosity at what the Book held in its pages.

A bit later, the two teens clapped their hands together in a slamming high five, did a man-hug pat on the back, and then parted for the night. William drug his feet in disappointment into the kitchen, where his mom and dad were preparing dinner. The food smelled a bit odd as he entered the kitchen, like a stinky shoe, but he kept that thought to himself. His dad was chopping an onion to help; but crying, for a man, is not the most sought-after response. *What a trooper,* William thought. He then gulped a glass of milk and peered into the living room. Mr. Wiker still sat hunched forward, eyes glued to the TV. William noticed the program was a fashion home channel advertising a special on bath rugs: only $19.95, and with a free toilet brush, if one called in the next fifteen minutes.

Above the well-worn, old man floated a dark angel, strong in appearance with a blade harnessed to its back, a blade mostly concealed by the cloak of gloom. The angel was cleaning his teeth with the tip of the dagger in its hand; it had a far, far different personality from the fragile man that sat in the chair below. William returned to the kitchen and sat in his seat, awaiting dinner with his face downcast and mind deep in thought. His dad walked up to him, placed his hands on his shoulders, and asked, "Is everything all right, William? You seem a little down."

"Dad, I need to share something with you. Could we talk on our own in the hall?" William requested, softly.

"Yes, of course," William's dad answered.

The two casually walked onto the hallway's wooden floors and William began to share words of wonder, up to now held in by a boy of few life experiences. William's dad spoke up first: "So, what's going on?"

"Dad, do you think there are demons?" William asked, shyly.

"Well, yes. Why do you ask?" William's dad spoke with surprise in his voice at his son's question.

William blurted out his story in one breath, staring just past his dad's eyes in a frozen sort of look as he shared his present reality.

"Well, I had this dream that I was struck by lightning, and it caused my eyes to only see in shadows of black and white. And everyone I see—in the dream that is—has an angel above them—either light or dark. At the end of the dream, it just flashes and I wake up. Do you think that's odd? You know, for a dream and all?"

His dad waited until William looked back in his eyes, informing him that William was finished recapping his so-called "dream."

His dad thought for a moment, contemplating how to give the most fitting response. "No, William. Dreams are just dreams. It's not weird. We can only control what our eyes see in the day. Like not watching scary movies," his dad said, looking at him and clearing his throat. "But, I wouldn't be too worried about it. Just remember, good triumphs over evil. Maybe not at first, but always in the end."

"Time to eat!" William's mom called from the kitchen.

"Come on," his dad said in a casual manner. "Let's go get Mr. Wiker and have some dinner. And remember, it's just a dream." William shrugged his shoulders at the end of his dad's talk; he was disappointed in the answer he had been given, wishing more than anything it was only a dream.

The two entered the living room. William's dad was coming to the realization that his son was growing into more of a man each day, and that he needed to start showing him how to approach various things. But how?

Mr. Wiker had his chin dropped to his chest, breathing heavily. "Mr. Wiker, time for dinner," William's dad said. There was no response from the wrinkled, aged man sitting before them. William's dad gently shook Mr. Wiker by his fragile shoulders, touching bones more than anything. Mr. Wiker woke with a grumble and mumble, saying, "Turn off the lights, Agatha!"

The eyelids of William's old neighbor slowly lifted and blinked in a flutter-like manner, fighting the lamp's light after a good nap.

The family gathered and sat at the table. Chicken and mashed potatoes sat on their serving platters as on porcelain clouds at the table. William's gaze traveled to and fro above those at the table: light, dark, dark. William wanted to ask so many questions, but to whom?

"Let's say grace," his dad said, lifting the palms of his hands to invite everyone to hold hands together during prayer. William's dad was to his right, at the head of the table. Mr. Wiker was to the left, at the foot of the table with William's mom across from him. They all bowed their heads . . . no one said anything. William and Mr. Wiker looked up and made eye contact, making William feel a bit uncomfortable. William quickly bowed his head once more to prevent any further awkwardnes.

The voices of his Dad's angel and Mr. Wiker's angel overlapped into an orchestra of grunge metal conversation. *"Power of three cannot easily be broken. Three shall be a sweet harmony of answers. Remain true to us and we will remain true to you, giving you freedom to be just as you are."* The angels were complimenting each other and growing darker with each word shared.

William did not realize his breathing was sounding more like a panic attack than normal inhaling and exhaling.

Then the voice of the soft dove's cooing from the trees wrapped the darkness into silence as a prayer poured out. *"Truth is shown in time to come, courage is yours, and strength is the ONE. . . . God is your all, Jesus is the way, be set free from this darkness cloak and be clothed in LIGHT."* William pulled away from contact with those beside him.

"So, is anyone going to pray?" Mr. Wiker asked in a failed attempt at a joke.

"Um, yeah!" William's dad said, looking at William, who broke the common holding-hand prayer formation. "William, would you like to say grace?" he asked.

"Shh . .. sh . . . sure," William said as he bowed his head for the third time. William tightened his face and closed his eyes as a child would after getting chlorine in his eyes from swimming. Slightly leaning his head forward, he prayed, "God . . ." There was a long moment of silence as William tried to think of the right words to say. "God, thank you for this food that my mom made. Thank you that Mr. Wiker can join us for dinner tonight. I pray that this food would nourish our bodies and that . . . I pray that everyone would know if their angel is light or dark." William quickly opened his eyes and looked up at his dad to explain. "I mean, like the dream," William said.

William's dad looked up, giving a puzzled, yet supportive, facial expression for William to continue. Mr. Wiker peeped open one eye to see if he could eat yet . . . *nope the kid was still mumbling on and on and on.*

William's mom softly smiled. "Go on dear," she said.

"I mean," William continued, "don't you ever wonder what kind of angel is above someone or above yourself?"

"You mean, like a guardian angel?" his dad asked, now also holding up the prayer from continuing.

"Well, yeah, like a guardian angel or like a demon or something," William added.

"What do you mean, 'demon?'" asked Mr. Wiker, suddenly amused at this conversation.

"Well, what if everyone has an angel above them?" William asked, trying to explain himself. "Like a good angel or a bad angel . . ."

"Like good and evil?" interrupted his dad.

"Yeah, like good and evil, but only one. I mean, only a good angel or only a bad angel," William said, now realizing that his body temperature was rising, and he felt like it was somewhere around 500 degrees. William thought he should have never opened his mouth. His mom should have prayed, not him!

"But everyone has a guardian angel," Mr. Wiker added, clearly not agreeing, and using a low tone of voice to convey his disagreement.

"No," William sharply responded, "not everyone has a light angel."

"Light angel?" asked Mr. Wiker, "You mean 'light' is 'good?'"Mr. Wiker's volume of voice was increasing and his eyebrows showing some fierceness—even from such a wrinkly face.

"Yes — " William said, but was quickly cut off by Mr. Wiker.

"And you mean to say that some people don't have a light angel? Are you saying I don't have a guardian angel? Are you trying to say that I am demon possessed?!"

"Ummm . . . ummm . . . I, I . . . I don't know!" William exclaimed, nervous now at the aggressive angel lunging to grab hold of him from above his old, hunched neighbor. William did not know the limit of these winged beings or their capabilities and quickly backed up out of reach. "No," he repeated, now looking at his dad, "I'm not saying that . . ." and now he was looking back at Mr. Wiker. "I didn't mean that you are possessed by a demon, Mr. Wiker. I was just saying that . . ."

"I'm sorry." Mr. Wiker spoke up once more, standing up

from his seat. "Thank you for inviting me to dinner, but now I must retire."

"Mr. Wiker," William's mom called out as she followed quickly behind him. "Mr. Winker, surely you can see that William was not trying to say those things about you."

Mr. Wiker politely shook his head as if to say he had had enough conversation for one night. "Thank you for letting me watch your TV," he said as he turned to leave.

Catching one final moment of eye contact with William, he mouthed a sentence that nearly made William collapse where he sat.

## CHAPTER EIGHTEEN

# Spill the Beans

It's an interesting concept, these things called dreams. . . . Are they the result of held-in desires or are they haphazard randomness that can't really be explained? The difference with William was that he was facing dream-like events in real life, and these did not end when he awoke from sleep—it was really just beginning. Each dream he dreamed when asleep provided an escape to a dream-filled reality of angels and demons being the true reflection of their eternal souls. Yet, William needed not a dream interpreter but a reality explainer.

William lay face down on his bed, arms by his side, nose smashed into the mattress. William did not respond to the knock at the door. William's dad knocked again as he entered the room. He walked up to his son, sat on the floor next to the bed, and placed a hand of comfort on his back. A haunted voice came with heat to William's heart: *"Power in the hands of the one you love, hold on to the questions and I will guide your way to the answers."*

"So, I see your Bible is no longer missing," his dad said, moving his hand from his back and trying to lighten the mood. "You know, William, before Grandpa passed away, he would read the Bible to me every night. I despised him for it. I didn't want to be told what to do. I wanted to be the one in charge of my life. Only now do I realize how wrong I was. I can't control anything. Not if it will rain tomorrow. Not if I will get a promotion at work. Not if I live or die. I want you to be different from me . . ."

William's dad gave a long pause to allow time for a response, but as his son remained on the well-folded blankets, he continued. "I believe you . . . you know, about seeing angels and demons." William sat up on his elbows and looked at his dad.

"You do?" William asked, monotone.

"I do. Could you tell me more about it?" William's dad asked. William could sense his dad's sincerity. William adjusted his posture and, now sitting cross-legged on the bed, leaned his elbows on top his knees.

"Dad, did you really despise Grandpa for reading the Bible to you?" William asked, surprised. William always thought his grandpa and dad got along, not that there was a battle of religion between them.

"Yes, William; I did. I wish it had not been the case, but there always was a wall in our relationship, and it was about God. And reading the Bible was just one of the bricks of that wall. I know your grandpa meant well but I felt like he was just pushing his beliefs on me." William's dad had spoken with much conviction, but now chose to change the topic. "So; about your dream?"

William decided there was no need to hide it, so he just spilled the beans. "OK, so what I know is that the night I spent at Blue Hill Forest began with me seeing in color, then a big flash of lightning came and blinded my eyes. When I woke up,

I could only see in black and white. Not only did my vision change to seeing in black and white, but I could see an angel hovering alongside or above everyone around me—either dark or light. So freaky! Like some sci-fi movie or something."

"Uhhuum," William's dad said, sitting still, his jaw dropped in disbelief. William continued with his steady stream of crazy events.

"Then, each angel carries armor and weapons, bows and arrows, swords, daggers, all old knights' stuff, it seems. I haven't figured out what the dark and light angels have in common—but I am saying to you right now, I don't think a dark angel is good. And dad, you and . . ."

Ring! . . . Ring! . . . The conversation point was cut off.

William reached for the phone and answered, "Hellowww."

The voice on the other end responded: "Hey buddy, I know you're probably still hanging out with Wrinkle Bottoms . . ."

William interrupted: "Hector, now's not a good time."

"O.K. I'll be quick. I am going to camp and Charles is going to be a counselor. Sweet or what?!" Hector said, pumped up with excitement.

"Yeah, cool. . . . Umm, can we talk later?" William said, half-excited, half-confused. Hector had never been to camp. Now the year he was planning on not going, his best friend signs up? "Alright... later," both said, then hung up.

Meanwhile, William's dad was curious as to what color his angel was, but he was honestly too scared to find out.

"I'm sorry," William said to his dad. "What were we saying?"

"Uum . . ." William's dad tried to think of the right words, "You were talking about dark angels and light . . ." his dad began to say, and then William quickly interrupted him, remembering where he had left off.

"Yeah, that's it! What light angels and dark angel have in common, right?"

"Right," his dad said, trying to convey the right demeanor to encourage William to continue. His dad did not know whether to believe his son's words or not. How could a thirteen-year-old child be able to see angels and demons? To know whether someone was going to Heaven or hell? Is that really what his son was saying? William's dad began to reflect on his own life; he did feel certainty, but not the kind of certainty of comfort in death. To his dad, the thought of forever… flames were not appealing in any way.

William was hesitant to speak. "So this dream' you were talking about," William's dad asked, "Was it really a dream or are you saying this really, really happened?"

"It really happened, Dad," William said softly while lying on the side of his bed. "Do you believe me?"

"Son, I . . ." William's dad was unable to get out what he wanted and so interrupted himself with a question. "So I guess Mr. Wiker's angel is not light?" His dad asked.

"Yeah, it's dark, like black-hole dark." William said, looking down at his hands to prevent eye contact.

"And your mom's angel is white, right?" he asked his son.

"Very bright," William said, now looking back up into his dad's eyes.

William's dad seemed deep in thought, inhaled strongly, and then asked, but with noticeable tentativeness, "And . . . your angel, William?"

"I hope to change this angel that hovers above me, but . . ." His dad nodded his head to encourage William to continue sharing. ". . . My angel's dark," William said, looking straight into his dad's eyes. His dad felt uncomfortable and looked away. "I guess like father, like son, right? William said with a half-smile, but his dad did not smile at all. His dad's heart dropped, looking down at his own hands as if to say, "It must be true."

"Dad," William called out as he began to cry softly. "I don't want a dark angel."

"Come here, William," his dad said, giving his best attempt

to console his son. William hugged his dad and wrapped his arms around his dad's neck. The father-son display of comfort looked as if William was trying to pull his dad onto his bed as his dad remained seated on the floor. All in all, it was quite the awkward comfort moment for such a serious situation. His dad began to cry, for the soul of his son, and he sobbed inwardly over the reality of his own. Both felt hopeless and scared. Suddenly, a voice like nails on a chalkboard spoke poetically into William's ears.

It was his dad's angel that shared new words of deception *"Unto you shall be fulfilled all your desires! Your life is to be as it is!"* Fear found William cringing and holding tightly to the arms of the one who was responsible for raising him. All William wanted to do was run from his dad's arms. William understood all too well that if his dad knew about his son's ability to hear these angelic voices, his dad would become unwilling to hug him—much less, touch him. How is it that this one act of compassion and physical touch could birth such unforeseen fears? William's dad still did not know for certain whether to believe his son's words or to view the comments as child-like imaginings. William's dad hoped for the second of the two.

William tried with all his might to keep from lessening his grip on his dad, despite his knowledge that these horrific yet beautiful voices would continue to dance in his ears. *"Build this bond between you and your dad. You are one and the same in flesh and desire. Seeking change of present form would tear apart this relationship with your father,"* continued the voice, like a soft waterfall. William's body remained natural and relaxed on the outside, but his mind was filled with dread; his dad held him ever so tightly. Hopelessness overtook both of them to silence.

Not knowing what else to say—after all, this was about their souls' eternal destinies—William's dad suggested, "Let's go finish up dinner. Don't want to go to bed on an empty stomach." William nodded in agreement. This had been enough talk on dark angels for one night. Both got up and walked toward the door as his dad held his son's shoulder again. "William, let's not tell your mom. She would only worry."

"Yeah," William spoke, as if a small burden of relief had been lifted. It felt nice not being alone with a secret such as this. Each pulled an immense amount of air into their lungs and both sighed strongly in unison. "Well, put on your happy face," William's dad said.

"Yep," William said.

William's dad patted his own cheeks with his hands to bring some color back to his face; the conversation seemed to have drained the blood from his face, and he was looking rather ill. Nonetheless, they entered the kitchen with a smile on their faces as William's mom sat at the dinner table with a cup of tea. All the plates had been cleared.

William was the first to break the silence. "Hey, could we try the dinner again, even though we lost a guest and I created the weirdest conversation ever?"

His mom played along as though everything was OK, even though she knew an issue was at hand. "Yeah, I was thinking you two would be back down. I have our food staying warm in the oven. Everything OK, William?" she asked softly, honestly.

"Yep, great. . . . Just needed a little guy time. Oh, and I want to go to camp this summer," William said, perhaps a little too much enthusiasm coming out in hopes of covering the burden placed on his heart.

"Camp? What got you to change your mind?" William's mom asked in surprise, although William had a tendency, as all young teens do, to change his mind often. William's mom reflected on a handful of other times William had changed his mind. The first memory was when William begged and begged to be a cowboy for Halloween when he was five. Then on Halloween, he saw an astronaut costume on TV and threw a fit until he put an empty water jug with eye holes cut out on his head. Another memory flashed of when William could not decide which shirt to wear. So he wore three to school. His mom lightly giggled at such memories. The family chatted over the reheated dinner and continued the conversation. The meal ended casually and good-nights were shared.

William's dad remained calm, outwardly, during his goodnight hug with his son as he whispered into his ear words he often forgot to say: "I love you." William's dad shared these words while on the verge of tears, choking on his own emotion. The darkness above his dad said, *"I love you too."*

"I know," William said calmly, nodding his head while felling full of gratefulness to finally hear an "I love you,"—but spooked by the demon angel saying the same thing in mockery.

William could not remember the last time his dad actually said the words "I love you." William would see his dad show acts of love, but the words always seemed to evaporate like water on an overheated highway.

William found the side of his bed once again, this time on his knees. "God . . ." A long pause followed with much folding and unfolding and refolding of hands, eyes open, eyes closed, and so forth. "Hi . . ." William hit his head with his palm, fumbling with how to address God in prayer. "Ummm, thanks for this day. . . . I don't want to have a dark angel. I don't want Dad to have a dark angel. I want to see in color again. I want to scream. I . . . I . . . just don't know. Amen."

He lay in bed and stared up at the black figure still residing above his head. "Don't you ever sleep?"

## CHAPTER NINETEEN

# Just Dreams or Not

Monday morning. William woke up to the sound of the ringing of the phone and looked at the alarm clock, which read 7:58 a.m. Rolling over on his bed to get more sleep, his mom knocked on the door. "William, Hector's on the phone."

"One minute," William said, stumbling out of bed and walking to the door. "Thanks," he said to his mom, grabbing the phone.

"Hello?"

"Wow! I can smell your morning breath through the phone!" Hector said, laughing.

"Hey, sorry I didn't call you back last night," William said.

"It's cool," Hector answered. "I just stayed up all night crying my eyes out, waiting for you to keep your word."

Knowing his best friend's sarcastic ways, William said, "Yeah,

I was too busy playing patty cake with Old Man Wiker on my top bunk." William's angel must have found this funny also, because he was laughing!

Hector laughed at this mental picture. "So, how was your date with Wrinkle Bottoms anyways?"

Looking toward the wall to avoid the creepy dude above his head, William exclaimed, "Horrible!"

"What?" Hector interrupted with a pouty voice. "Did you get stood up again?"

"No, really," William continued, "It went horrible. I prayed . . ."

"You prayed! Oh no!" interrupted Hector once more.

"Come on, man," William said, requesting that Hector not interrupt. "I prayed that people would know if their angel is light or dark."

"You know, a wise man once said that 'It don't matter if you're black or white,'" Hector said, singing these lyrics.

"I don't think he was referring to angels, Hector," William clarified.

"So what did Whiney-Carrot say?" asked Hector.

"He thought I was saying he was demon-possessed," William replied.

"Duhhh. Of course he is!" replied Hector. William was quiet for a moment.

"Well, he is," William finally thought. William shook his head, thinking, *I hope that's not the case with me.*

"Hello? Anybody there?" Hector said to William. "Did I offend you, William?"

"No," William softly said. "It's just that . . . Hector, I really think I can see them."

"Yeah, me too," Hector responded, lying, "Who can't see them?"

William did not like Hector dismissing what he was trying to share.

"I'm just joking, man," Hector confessed. "You're just . . . really weird, you know that? I guess I'll still be your best friend and all, but don't go getting all spiritual on me like Charles does. . . . So, can you play today, or what?"

"Who says 'play?'" William asked, poking fun of Hector's wording for a change.

"OK then," Hector said, injecting some humor, "Can you hang out with your homey?"

William now laughed in response, "Yeah, yeah, G-thug. I'll ride to your crib after I grub. But I have to ask my mom first."

"OK. Call me later," Hector said. The darkness above William still held a smile, his daggers tucked away in his side harness strap, hovering inches from the ground instead of the favorite above-the-head position.

William decided to join the smiling, but for another reason completely, and he spoke the reason out loud:

"Jesus Christ."

The two words sent the darkness to shriveling vapors—and then it vanished completely.

William closed his eyes and fell back asleep, reaching REM mode in what seemed like only seconds. William's sleep was deep, but his dreams unpleasant: Thunder and lightning filled the room as his body twitched from the dreams. A flash of lightning filled William's room with a strobe-like effect of light as William tossed and turned. Then, multiple visions: the first of swords clanging and dark and light angels fighting heavily. Sweat formed on William's neck and above his eyebrows. Restaurant images surrounded him. He was hearing the voice of Penny's angel as it spoke dark and evil words to her.

He was wondering how to tell Penny that she had a dark angel that spoke constant lies of destruction to her soul. How do you share truth without hurting someone? The kind of truth that will inevitably hurt? How do you help and yet keep from adding hurt to this horrid reality of one's eternal soul which is struggling to keep from struggling?. . . A flash of his dad playing catch with him in the front yard. Grandpa is there at the picnic table, but all is not the same as it once was. Dad's angel is there: Dark. William can see his grandpa's angel: Light. Heavy breaths begin exiting William's nose and mouth. He is listening to a conversation between himself and Charles, in which Charles was asking him if he believes in God. They were at the Epsilon Eatery. Charles sat. Two angels stood above him, both white angels, fully armed.

Oblivious William was on the day these events began, but he now vividly saw the scene from a distance, both the angels above Charles and that of his own angel. His angel kneeling and crying as Charles's angel held steady both arms, reaching out over the darkened form. As Charles shared God's name out loud, darkness shuttered. Another lightning sparked and thunder roared. William's dream flashed to a picture that hung in his grandparent's house, positioned above the sofa. He read it every time he visited. The picture was of Jesus building a house. Jesus has well-tanned skin and is strong in appearance, with children standing, watching in joy. A verse at the bottom of the picture read: "Psalm 37 – 'The salvation of the righteous comes from the Lord, He is their stronghold in times of trouble. The Lord helps them and delivers them. He delivers them from the wicked and saves them, because they take refuge in Him.'"

The picture fades into complete darkness. He sees a boy running in a field of wild flowers with a shadow following close behind the boy. The shadow is growing in size and consuming all the color of the field, and now forming wings as a sword becomes evident in its hand. The boy looks back . . . William recognizes the boy. . . . the boy was himself—fleeing as prey from a predator. He felt heat spread over his body, attempting to burn him, when the thunder roared in the dream and it woke him up to the reality of living in a nightmare. For once, he wished his dreams didn't come true.

## CHAPTER TWENTY

# Soggy Toes

Startled, William awoke abruptly, grabbing his chest, gasping as if trapped underneath waves, and unable to find the surface of the water. William looked at the clock. 8:32a.m. *Bang*! William jumped and looked out the window. It was the trash truck pickup service, and it was not so gently compacting the neighborhood trash. William rolled his eyes. "Monday," he said, as he slammed his head back onto the pillow, covering his face with his hands. He forced his sluggish arms to throw the covers off violently, and he felt better at taking his anger out on the cotton comforter.

William walked downstairs to the kitchen for breakfast. His mom was walking from the garage to a room upstairs and then back into the garage once more, each time carrying a box full of something in her hands. "Morning, honey," his mom said to William as she held his face and kissed him on the cheek while balancing a box in her other hand. The soothing voice of her angel greeted his ears: *"Strength given in prayer, guidance in Scriptures read."*

"Good morning." William smiled; it felt cozy to him when her angel spoke. This was especially needed after such an awful night of rest. "What's in all those boxes, Mom?" William asked.

"Oh, just a lot of top-secret files from Sector Eleven," she replied with a mother-like smile, as if to say, "I'm not going to tell you."

"Ha. I thought you moved to Sector Thirteen a few months back," William joked. "Is Dad home?"

"No, he left for work fifteen minutes ago," she replied. "So are you excited about your big day tomorrow? The big one-four?" his mom asked as she carried her final box to the van.

"Oh yeah! I can't wait!" William exclaimed, faking enthusiasm with a fist bump to the ceiling.

"Do you want to go to your favorite restaurant again?" asked his mom.

"I was thinking we could just stay home and have grilled chicken and cheesy potatoes... and have a sleepover with Hector and Michael and Austin?" asked William with something like big ol' puppy eyes.

"Barbeque chicken on the grill sounds great, but you leave for camp the next morning. You won't be able to have a sleepover. Maybe some other time," his mom replied.

"But mom, it's my birthday!" William begged.

"And camp is your birthday present," his mom said, keeping firm with her decision.

"Then can I have Hector over for dinner and sleep at his house?" William asked. "Please? Charles can take me to camp then!"

"I will talk with your dad when he gets home," his mom replied. "OK," William said in a respectful, and yet bummed tone of voice.

"Can I go to Hector's after breakfast?" William asked.

"I don't see why not, but we have to make two stops first, one of which is some shopping for your early birthday presents."

William was playing "Mom's mannequin game" from store to store, until the show-and-tell was over and peace was found at Hector's front door. William never liked shopping and was reminded of that fact all the more after their three-hour tour.

William stood at the front door, he could hear faint footsteps quickening in pace and volume. Eight seconds later, the door opened and Hector splashed the biggest bucket full of water on William's chest, drenching the entire front of his body. The door slammed shut and William stood frozen outside, iced over by the chilled water. Three seconds later, the door swung open again as Hector and Charles threw two pounds of baking powder at William, turning him into a pasty white ghost. Once more, the door slammed shut and William was left alone outside, standing in a snowsuit of white powder. He turned toward his mom seated in the van, smiled really big, waved his hand in the air, and yelled, "Bye Mom! See you at four o'clock!"

His mom shook her head side to side and backed out of the driveway, leaving her son to clean up the white powdered mess. This had been the third flouring in three weeks. Hector and Charles swung the door open a final time. William threw his hands up to cover his face as the two boys picked him up and wrestled him to the ground in the front yard. Two voices—one dark, one light—took hold of the opportunity to share their voices. Charles' angel of light spoke calmly, although Charles himself was body-slamming William in the yard.

"Share your questions and answers will be shown, Charles will help you walk to the way narrow." But Hector's gloomy angel provided mere harassment.

"Lies you speak, what do you offer? I offer the world and all that's in it, just let me keep you mine." The next-door neighbor who was push mowing his yard became so distracted from witnessing these weird teenagers having fun that he mowed over his wife's prized flowers. The three boys tried to stop laughing, but failed miserably as William ineffectively wiped the white patchy paste off his moist skin, smudging it all the more.

"So, how was shopping?" Charles asked in a girly voice.

"Torture!" William replied. "We walked around in the mall for three hours and tried on like fifty pairs of clothes."

"Did you see any cute girls?" asked Hector, the girl-crazy one of the group.

"I saw Penny," William said with a romance type of voice.

"Did you toot her another love song?" Hector asked.

"No, even worse!" William admitted. "I was trying on some jeans at Carcel's and my mom did the little 'Want to check if your britches fit your little hiney' thing. You know, how moms check the waistband and tug on them like it's going to loosen them? While my Mom starts tug-tugging on the pant leg, Penny was standing like ten feet from me, staring straight at my hips, then my eyes, and back at my hips again! Ooooh! I pushed my mom's hand and ran into a rack full of shirts."

Hector and Charles were cracking up laughing as Charles retried the pant tug on Hector, shaking his little brother's pants and saying, "You have any poo-poo in your dipe-dipes?" They all laughed.

"After that," William continued, "we went to FLP and the same thing happened again! I was trying on a pair of khaki pants and my mom goes to reach toward my hips and says,

'Lift up your shirt a little.' So I lift my shirt up and look to my right. There's Penny! Ten feet away! Again! Staring right at my hips! This time my mom screams 'Aaahhh!' because I wedged four rubber spiders around my waist. Ha! Ha! Ha! This time, she turns and runs into the empty clothes hanger rack!"

"What did Penny do?" asked Charles.

"I don't know," William said. "I was too distracted at my

mom yelling at me. I didn't see her again." The boys had tears in their eyes and were holding their sides from the laughter of William's once-again-embarrassing moment with Penny. If there had been any hope of Penny liking William, it had now been set on fire, crushed, broken, and buried in the Saudi Arabian desert, never to be seen again. William kept a good attitude when sharing the day, but there was no question he was sad. He really liked Penny and did not want to always be seen as a fool.

"So, you want to borrow some clothes or do you need your mom to help you change your pants?" asked Hector in a baby talk manner, making a motion of pretend tears.

"Hey," William said, running toward Hector, trying to tackle him to the ground. The boys managed to make it to the backyard. They had a water hose attached to the side wall as a makeshift shower. This is highly necessary when you have teenage boys, especially ones that enjoy messy activities—as these boys did.

William was the last to get in the water to rinse off. By now the baking soda was like cement, sealing in a smile on his face. Hector ran upstairs to grab William some clothes. William took off his shirt and rinsed it in a steady, yet chilly stream of water. His attention was fully given over to getting the red cotton shirt free from the snow that became entangled in its fibers. Unaware of the procession of tiny footsteps making their way up the driveway, William began singing out loud, humming at first, then growing steadily louder as he twisted the shirt to dispense the water to assist it in its drying.

Then he began singing: "I want to stand with you on a hill top. I want to ride my bike in the park. I want to hold your hand forever . . . oh Penny, oh oh, la de da de da da da ohhh!" The steps grew closer as William sang louder, and then picked up a garden shovel that was propped up in a pale beside the porch, and used it as a microphone. He continued with his revised favorite song: "And when I see you Penny in the diner or department store, I make a wish up to Heaven and make us want to smile. It's a newww beginning . . . a reeeeeason for living, if only . . ."

William's musical performance was cut short as he turned to the sound of tiny, non-boy giggles. Penny and three of her friends were standing—that's right, Penny—ten feet away, fully entertained by William's singing. William, shirtless, wet, hair spiked up, holding a garden shovel, and with a face still forming the word "only" on his lips, stood wide-eyed in shock at yet another moment of embarrassment.

"Hi, William," Penny said, greeting him with a smile. "Trying out for the talent show?" Penny asked, chuckles escaping her mouth. William was surprised out of his socks—that is, if he had had any to hop out of.

"Uh, hey girls. What's up?" his voice cracked.

The door opened on the back porch. Hector ran out: "Hey got the . . ." Hector shouted, and then cut himself off when he saw the garden full of cute ladies. William turned the water spigot off at the wall while trying to flex all of his muscles, though all of that did not amount to much more than a red face. Then he walked toward Hector, who had clothes and a towel in his hands.

"So, you boys busy?" asked a short Asian girl from Penny's posse. Hector, being of the "I am not shy" type, tossed the handful of clothes to William and strolled on over to the half-circle of dazzling, delicate school girls. Two of them, however, looked quite bored.

Hector spoke as deeply as his best puberty voice could take him: "No, our busyness ends when beauty walks in." Penny's eyes were locked on William, who was fumbling to get another shirt on. He decided to not change his soaked shorts, for he was not going to make a scene in his boxers in front of such a rare sunflower. Maybe he would be cool and make up for the awkwardness at the mall.

"Why are you all wet?" another girl asked William.

"Oh, just wrestling an alligator in the backyard. It's a good work out. Gotta' watch out for their tails, though . . . tough they are. Throw you across the street if you get too close," William spoke, sarcastically and yet cool, surprised at the quick wit he had been able to conjure up. Even the girls laughed and giggled some at those lines.

Hector's smile dimmed as his eyes moved to his best friend. Hector was usually the one getting the girl's attention. Who was this stealing the spotlight? The door again swung open. This time Charles entered the scene with a Super Soggy 2000, a high-powered water gun, loaded with H2O. He unleashed a water stream with enough pressure, right on William's back, to send him forward, falling on his knees to the grass. The girls received the aftershock of the water bouncing off William's back, as sprinkles of water were now flying their way. The girls now revealed their hands—which had been conveniently placed behind their backs—with mini water guns, two for each girl, now aimed at the boys.

"Let the battle begin!" shouted Hector with a battle-like cry, throwing his fist into the air. Charles was in charge of the house today, for their mom was out grocery shopping. *Such discipline Charles has*, thought William as he ran for cover behind the stainless steel grill, watching Hector sprint to the garden hose at the wall. The girls traveled in a pack, forming a wall of tiny water squirts that were sent flying in William's direction. These tiny, squealing girls still looked like flowers, despite their so-called aggressive battle charge.

William peeped over the grill and saw Penny running away. He then stood up straight, wondering were Penny was going. She disappeared behind the corner of the house, only to reappear with a Super Soggy 3000 Turbo, twice the size of the one Charles had, which he now realized was almost empty. Penny full-sprinted toward defenseless William, who was now completely vulnerable. William found himself smiling—standing with open arms as if to receive a big hug—only to be pelted with a shower of water that collided into his face and neck. Once again, William slipped to his rear onto the grass.

This little flower garden of girls traveled behind the leader of their bloom brigade. Charles and Hector filled their empty squirt guns as the skies continued to open up—and none of it coming from rain. Soaked from head to toe twice over, all, now with empty water guns, decided the battle was over and sought peace in this backyard.

As the kids all laughed, William took Penny by the hand and slipped away behind the garden house.

## CHAPTER TWENTY-ONE

# Who Knew?

"So, umm, how long have you been in the SGM?" William asked Penny.

"SGM? What's that?" Penny asked William, head tilted, clearly confused.

"You know," replied William. "Squirt Gun Mafia? It's kind of a big thing."

"Oh," Penny said, playing along with William's horrible flirting abilities. "SGM. I actually left that group in '07 and started my own. Yeah, we're called the SQUAKS!" Penny said, now providing her best, Mafia-like impression.

"SQUAKS?" William asked. "Like a goose?"

Penny shook her head yes and seemed to have the loveliest smile that William had ever seen.

"So, I guess that is like an acronym for Squirt Queens Under

Attack Kiss . . ."Oh no! William had just said the K-word! Penny's eyes shot wide open. William straightened up and said, "I mean, Attacking Knight Squad." Penny smiled some more as William's face turned three shades of red.

"We actually don't have an acronym yet," Penny said in an attempt to continue the conversation in an upbeat way, playfully ignoring the K-word that had been shared. "But as the god-mother of the SQUAKS Mafia, I could propose your acronym for consideration to the group at our next meeting." William looked over at Hector and Charles, who were entertaining the other SQUAKS Mafia members by the back patio. Charles was running after Hector in a circle, throwing water balloons and baking powder at him, though the baking powder was mostly getting on Charles, himself. The girls were sitting and laughing amongst each other, oblivious to the fact that William was wooing Penny with his acronymical abilities.

"What's the name of your mafia?" asked Penny.

"Oh, I'm not in one," William said, not picking up on the hint that Penny really wanted to continue the conversation. Penny smiled as she waited for William to respond. "We're called the . . ." William looked around the backyard, trying to think of something to say as an acronym. ". . . the PBJ."

"PBJ?" Penny asked, utterly confuse by that one.

"Yeah, ummm . . . Powerful Baking Powder Judges," William replied.

"Where does the second P come from?" Penny asked, calling out William's error. "Um,mm it's silent—so that we can fit in other types of baking goods." William was taken back at his own quick thinking. Yeah, sometimes we use powder, sometimes marshmallows, sometimes spaghetti noodles, and sometimes mashed potatoes."

Penny laughingly said, "But only after baked, right?"

"Yeah, of course!" William responded, casually.

"By the way," Penny said to William, "Happy early birthday."

"Thanks, Penny," William said. "It means a lot. But . . . how did you know that tomorrow's my birthday?"

"Hector's older brother told us when he saw us on the sidewalk, before he gave us the squirt guns," Penny admitted.

"I see. Then, I guess, thanks for the gift of super-soaking me clean." William gestured toward his soggy shirt and matted powdered hair. "I'm having a birthday dinner at my house tomm . . ."

"Oh, I won't be able to go," Penny interrupted. "I'm leaving for camp the next morning." William's heart jumped. Could it be true? Was fate bringing these two together to spend five entire days together at camp? Or was it God? At that moment, William thought that God's hand was in everything, or at least he liked to think so when the situation seemed to benefit him.

"Really, you're going too?!" William asked Penny.

"Yeah, I went last year, but I . . . wait. *Too?* Are you going to camp, William?"

William did not know that Penny went to the same camp last year. Then again, William did not act as if girls existed until eleven months ago, when Penny and four of her friends sat down with him during school lunch. William thought they were going to date or something until the next day when he saw Penny and those same girls sitting with some other guy who was sitting all by himself. Penny was nice, from-the-heart-kind-of-nice, and William liked her. She was the only popular girl who was friends with everyone. That's why it was so unnerving for him to see her with a dark angel . . . when she was so nice to everyone.

"Yeah, I'm going too! And so is Hector and Charles!"

"Well, cool," Penny said.

"Cool? . . . Yeah, cool," William said, trying to calm his excitement, although he figured he said the word cool one too many times.

"A piece of advice," Penny said to William, who was suddenly all ears. "Make sure you don't sit on any more chocolate bars." William covered his face to hide his suddenly pink cheeks. "Come on, William," Penny said, playfully taking hold of his arm. William instantly heard her angel speaking again sharing breath, vile as sulfur: *"Seek this one in beauty's form. To gaze upon her love unborn. If you would give me your heart, her care for you shall never part. Your soul to me could be arranged. You two will never be estranged."*

The angel blew kisses towards William as he pulled away from Penny's grip and sat frozen on the grass, staring straight at Penny, who sensed that something was wrong.

Penny apologized. "William, I'm sorry, I was just joking. I didn't mean to . . ."

"You're fine," William interrupted Penny. "It's OK. I knew you were joking. I mean, you're like the nicest girl at school." Penny sat emotionless this time, for she did not know how to take genuine complements from others. William continued: "You're the girl that everyone wants to be. I mean, that every . . . *girl* wants to be, your bold and smart." William noticed though that Penny seemed distant from this latest compliment. "Penny?" William tried to get Penny to make eye contact. "Do you think you're pretty?"

She did not say anything. Penny looked down at the grass, looking as though she wanted to cry, shaking her head softly "*no*".

"Because, I think you are pretty, prettier than the baking soda masterpiece made of me," William added in the sweetest, most honest, and yet daring voice ever.

She snuffled her nose and wiped her eyes. "You mean fabulous Flour art."

William's mind was ready to share at least one meaningful conversation before he lost another opportunity to his foolish self. So he did with intent and purpose.

"If you knew a dark secret about someone else and sharing

it could either make it worse or better.....would you tell them?"

"Depends..." She paused wadding for the right words. "...if you loved them enough to share the truth in love."

She then stood up and said with a polite smile, "I'll see you at camp."

"Yeah, see you at camp," William said, contemplating how to tell this tale.

Penny and her friends exchanged a few words and began to walk away. Penny quickly turned and yelled, "Happy birthday, William!"

"Thanks, Penny!" William responded, with heartfelt emotion.

The girls skipped off toward the direction they had first come until their tiny brown and blonde locks were out of sight.

The boys did a chest bump and a big "Yeah" in a loud voice. Hector asked, abruptly, "Hey, you want to camp out tonight?"

"Yeah! Got to ask my dad, though," said William, still overjoyed inside at his exchange with Penny. Inside, William felt like flying.

"It won't be a real campout in the woods, but in our backyard. We can have a bonfire and some mellows of course, burnt or golden, raw or none," Charles added, using a southern drawl.

"Y'all can tell spooky stories and drink root beer 'til the cow jumps the moon," Hector added in a funny cowboy lingo.

The next seventeen hours flew by.

## CHAPTER TWENTY-TWO

# Time Tickers

*F**lash forward...*

| | |
|---|---|
| 3:30 pm | Called mom. Begged and pleaded to sleep at Hector's. Continuing to remind her that tomorrow was his birthday. |
| 3:41 pm | Mom says yes to campout. |
| 4:00 pm | Continued to hoop and howler about the recent flirting successes with the girls, and especially with Penny. |
| 4:02 pm | Hector slaps William on the backside and wrestles him to the ground until he says, "Uncle, mercy, uncle." |
| 4:25 pm | Begin to set up camp. Tent pole slaps William in face, then in shin, then wrist, then another final |

| | |
|---|---|
| | slap to the back of his head before the tent falls to a disastrous mess on the ground. Charles decides to put tent together on his own. |
| 5:40 pm | Charles' and Hector's mom arrives with groceries in hand, boys help, giggling and laughing for no apparent reason. |
| 6:03 pm | Collect sticks from yard to put by the campfire. Charles' and Hector's dad laughs at the two-inch pile of twigs, brings the boys a real log from garage, boys thank and praise dad, then high-five each other. |
| 6:35 pm | Charles' mom opens porch door, announces dinner, boys sprint inside, Charles casually walks behind, mom points to sink, boys wash hands, splash each other in the pants with water, William turns red-faced for the fortieth time in one day. It must be a new record for embarrassing moments in one day. |
| 6:41 pm | Charles laughs at William and Hector for the display of water-stained pants, then shouts, "Next time don't wait so long to use the loo!" |
| 6:42 pm | Parents see boys giggle to themselves as mom pretends it's not funny and acts mature by looking away. |
| 6:50 pm | William realizes angels are all white except Hector's and William's. William ponders for millionth time how to make his angel white. |
| 6:55 pm | Small talk about the day, sharing what they learned, what they're confused about, what they're excited about, jokes exchanged, plates clang, food eaten, shin kicks exchanged under the table. |
| 7:45 pm | Dishes being taken to sink, rinsed and placed in dish washer, each person returns to table when |

| | |
|---|---|
| | finished, chatting until all has been finished with eating. |
| 8:00 pm | Parents give advice about the campout: "Don't run from bears, don't light farts on fire, eat marshmallows responsibly, don't set the yard or tent on fire, have fun." |
| 8:08 pm | Nodding heads in agreement and in unison, boys smile brightly at the comical parental advice, realizing these are all the things they wanted to do. |
| 8:10 pm | Running up the stairs to borrow more clothes, William grabs Hector's pants, pulls his drawers down, Hector falls up the steps in push-up style. |
| 8:12 pm | Hector regains pants and footing and kicks the bottom of William's barefoot, in the upstairs hallway. William grumbles and grabs his own toe from bad decision for not wearing shoes. Yelps "Oh, man!" |
| 8:15 pm | After smelling shirts and shorts, boys manage to find some clothes for William. |
| 8:35 pm | Outside on a lawn chair, William reclining and stares at the only star visible from within a well-lit neighborhood backyard. Two sticks have flaming marshmallows—one Hector's and one Charles's—then they fall permanently in the flames . . . small jokes and stories and re-thinking what to do next time when girls show up. |
| 9:00 pm | Suddenly . . . heavy burden on William's heart, decides he must tell these guys what is really going on with his vision. |
| 9:04 pm | "I have a dark angel." William said in his exhale, feeling a tiny relief already. |

| | |
|---|---|
| 9:06 | "What are you turning into? Dark Vador?" Hector said, fully amused. |
| 9:07 | Charles was not so skeptical and confidently shared. "I believe in guardian angels." |
| 9:09 | Hector scoffed his smart mouth back at his brother. "You would believe in pretend child's play, you always have." |
| 9:12 | Charles' conviction compelled him to continue: "Just because you can't see angels, doesn't make them less real. I can't see the wind…but I can see the effects of the wind in small breezes moving leaves or entire neighborhoods flattened from a tornado. God is real and worth respecting, I fear him in his power. I know nothing happens without God allowing it. A God so loving, we truly cannot fathom." |
| 9:18 | "Yes…. I am starting to get that," William shared after much intense listening, desiring greatly to know what Charles knows. |
| 9:19 | "Whatever. You both sound preachy to me," replied doubtful Hector. |
| 9:35 pm | William shares detail after detail with Hector and Charles. "No way!" after "No way!" comes from the pair, until the whole story, every detail, has been exposed from his thumpingly nervous heart. |
| 9:38 pm | Silence captures the backyard; boys unsure what to do or say next. |
| 9:40 pm | Charles, as the older male, steps up to the challenge at hand, speaking slowly, calmly, unwavering, and delivers the following: "What do you know, William, about your dark angel?" |
| 9:42pm | Silence again floods the tiny grassed yard. It seems like infinity before William can speak |

about the disaster of confusion inside: "I got to turn to the light or I will die! But I don't know how." Hector, meanwhile, remained fully entranced with the third marshmallow set on fire at the tip of his stick.

Charles begins sharing the story of Christ: "Jesus came as a baby, grew up without ever sinning; Jesus was God's only son and God gave a promise that whoever . . . whoever believes in Jesus will not die eternally, but have everlasting life."

William jumped in adding his two cents. "I know about Jesus and his birthday being on Christmas and that he came back from the dead on Easter, I have been to church you know."

Charles was glad he could move on to the main subject rather than detouring with the background story. "Hearing the story and believing the story are two very different concepts," Charles said calmly, realizing this decision of faith would affect his eternity.

"William, we are all sinners, we all do what is not right. We need someone to release us of this burden of sin. Nothing that we can do by our own hands will allow us to be right with God. Jesus came on our behalf to not do wrong, to forgive us from sin, to be blameless and pure, to die as a perfect sacrifice for us all, once for all, past sin, current sin, and future sin."

William breathes deeply and asks: "I thought there was just Jesus and He was God. How does he have a father?"

Charles continues ... in confidence and elegant speech given fully by the Holy Spirit. " ... So a good way that helps me to grasp the concept of the Trinity is this: water can be in three states of being: a solid, a liquid, and gas. All remain water, the great H2O, and just appear in different forms. God is fully Jesus, who is fully the Holy Spirit, who is three-in-one. Each one is given a role according to the ultimate will of God the Father. Jesus even submits His will to the will of God. There are even things that God the Father only knows ... such as the second coming of Christ; only God knows the exact time. The Holy Spirit is the tool used to remain in saved hearts to help guide and direct those walking by faith, not by sight."

Meanwhile, Hector allows the marshmallow to sluggishly fall into the twelve-inch pit, then turns to face the conversation he was not so interested in.

"So should I get baptized or something? I want to go to Heaven," William asked, shyly.

"No, baptism is just a way to show others that you are now a follower of Christ. There is no 'holy water,' or magical act. Baptism is a great way to let others see your heart change," Charles said as he leaned on his knees poking the fire embers. Charles went on: "Being a Christian is realizing that Jesus is Lord, He died, and He rose to life three days later to forgive our sins so we may have a restored relationship with God.

"If we believe this to be true: that Jesus is Lord,

ruler of all, forgiver of our sins, then you will be saved from hell. Your life will have purpose and your death will be your return to God in Heaven. Jesus gave us grace."

"Who is . . . grace?" William asked.

"It's not a *who*. . . say you're speeding down the road and a cop pulls you over. He says, 'I will not give you a ticket although you deserve one. Have a nice day.' Now, that's mercy. Say you're speeding down another road and the cop pulls you over to give you a ticket and he says, 'I am not going to give you a ticket even though you deserve one, and I will give you 100 dollars because I can.' That's grace. Receiving the amazing gift of eternal life, without receiving the just punishment we do deserve of hell."

William was still confused about the whole baptism thing. "So, then I should get baptized, right?"

Charles had kind of forgotten about the whole baptism question and tried to clarify William's request. "When Jesus was nailed to the cross with nails in his wrists and feet, there were two men beside him. One man cursed Jesus and died; the other said that Jesus had done nothing wrong to deserve punishment, and he admitted that his own sins deserved punishment. After that, Jesus promised the second man that he would be with Jesus in Heaven. All three men hung on the cross. The one man that was promised to go with Jesus to Heaven didn't have time to go in a pool or lake to get baptized but he still went to Heaven. He was saved from sin because

Jesus could hear his confession of sincerity, one in which we can't save ourselves. It's not about . . ."

10:10 pm  "Make a wish," Hector blurted out as his digital watch displayed "10:10 p.m." on the face. William, too overwhelmed with the conversation present to care, ignored the make-a-wish comment.

10:12 pm  William got up and stretched his back. "Thanks for not thinking I am crazy, guys," William said, almost yawning.

10:13 pm  "Who said we didn't?" Hector blurted. "You're definitely crazy, William, but you were all that before this lightning, angel, dark and light jazz showed up, and you always will be. That's why we like you so much." Hector was trying to lighten the mood immensely.

10:15  "William, I am always available for conversations like this," Charles said as a last statement to repeat the importance of finding the answer about salvation.

10:17 pm  "Teeth-brushing time." William pulled the plastic bag from his pocket on his shorts and found a blue toothbrush inside.

"What in the world? Why do you have a toothbrush in your pocket?" Hector interjected, suddenly.

"Always be prepared, my dad always likes to say," William answered.

"Your dad doesn't always say that . . . the Boy Scouts do," Hector called back, pushing William into a flower bush.

10:20 pm  All three boys were using the outdoor faucet to

|  |  |
|---|---|
|  | brush their teeth. This is a far more manly way to do it, of course. |
| 10:32 pm | Re-arranging the tent to comply with all three boys' ideas of proper sleeping bag placement. |
| 10:42 pm | Still arguing over who gets to sleep by the door. Sleeping bags a pretzel mess on the floor. |
| 10:48 pm | Decision reached. Charles by the door, Hector in the middle, William on the farthest wall. |
| 10:53 pm | All lying on backs facing the netting-only ceiling. The shadows of the trees canopy their tent with the sliver of moon shining between the leaves as their nightlight. Arms positioned behind the head for Charles. Hector's arms by his sides, and William with one hand under his pillow and the other on his chest. |
| 10:59 | Goodnight punches exchanged. "Goodnights" announced, eyelids closed, minds continue pondering. Charles tries to finish were he left off with the Good News speech and says, "If you want to have this discussion again some time, I would be more than willing to do so." |
|  | "Enough with the spiritual whoop-la ... let's get some rest already," Hector said, rolling his eyes yet again over his older brother's proselytizing. "I appreciate it, Charles," William chimed back. |
| 11:12 pm | First twitches occur, Charles already sleeping with heavy-slumber breaths. |
| 11:21 pm | Hector follows suit, muscles firing the last of their energy inside Hector's blue and gray sleeping bag. |
| 11:40 pm | Still no sleep finding William's exhausted body. |
| 11:45 pm | A big, stinky fart exits his best buddy, making William want to cry from the sting of the smell. |

| | |
|---|---|
| 11:48 | William, still recovering from the poisonous gases, holds his nose shut with one hand and fans the air up to the exposed night sky, tainting something outside rather than his own nose. |
| 12:00 am | After the tent regains the fresh-cut grass scent which was so pleasant to William, he falls asleep ... |
| 12:02 am | Charles repositions body away from the door; creating a domino effect for Hector to move in the same direction. William, now finally unconscious, remains still on his back, both hands under his head, on his belly, head turned away from the zippered door. |
| 4:00 am | A rustle at the tent awakens Hector. Hector sits up, looks around with blurry, sleeping eyes and can see, silhouetted in the glow of the porch light, a hairy-tailed creature scratching the nylon fabric. |
| 4:01 am | He hits the other boys awake, too scared to say anything. Hector stands up as if he is actually going to do something about the situation. He peers over to peek through the netting to catch a glimpse of this frightening animal attacking their humble abode. With some disappointment, and yet relief, Hector looks into the eyes of a raccoon, who had been preoccupied digging in the remains of the trash by the fire. "Whoow," Hector exhales. "Only a raccoon. OK. Night-night." Then he laid back in his sleeping bag. |
| 4:08 am | William and Charles look at each other, shrug, and fall back off to sleep. |
| 6:00 am | The sun begins to break the darkness, blanketing the cloth that has been so much like home, |

so quietly situated in the corner of the yard. Sun pours into the eyes of three unsuspecting sleepers. It is morning—but not according to their body clocks.

## CHAPTER TWENTY-THREE

# Double Breakfast

Charles was the first to arise: he unzipped the tent, grabbed the bottom of William's and Hector's sleeping bags, and with one mighty tug both boys were dragged from the tent, squealing like piglets. When their roller coaster ride came to a halt, William and Hector wormed their little cocoon bodies back toward the tent for some more shut eye.

"Oh, no you don't!" exclaimed Charles, now jumping onto the bottom of their sleeping bags. "Mush! Mush! Onward, Willworm! Yah! Yah! Hec-turtle!" Charles said, riding his brother and holding onto William's sleeping bag.

"Come on, man," begged Hector, "get off!"

"Need! More! Sleep!" added William, still attempting to crawl away.

"No way, little birthday boy!" Charles said, remembering

what day it was.

"Oh, that's right!" Hector said as he crawled out of his sleeping bag and jumped on top of William, still fully enveloped inside.

"Time for some birthday spankings!" Hector declared, now trying to hold William down. With William face down, Charles straddled his shoulders and held down his arms. Hector sat on William's legs and began the birthday spanking to his now-fourteen-year-old cocooned best friend. "Uno, Dos, Twah," Hector yelled with each slap to William's sleeping bag-covered bottom.

"No! Stop! You're as big as a moose," laughed William, still trying to break free from Charles' grip. William could maybe have kept from laughing if his connection with angel and demon conversations could be placed on hold, but unfortunately, he did not know how to do so . . . The angel roared in William's ears:

*"Another year mine, another wonderful delightful year, make a wish and I will make it come true, who needs the light when you enjoy the night!"* William, unable to move, simply held still, waiting for this not-so-fun game to end.

Hector continued in his broken French numbering system: "Intercept, wheaties, nine, ten, eleven!" The spankings grew stronger. "Twelve, thirteen, and fourteen!" Hector said, now with hands pumping into the air as if he just made a soccer goal. Hector tumbled over to the grass as William finally wiggled out of his sleeping bag, now holding his backside.

"Yes! That's it, William. You are now a butterfly!" Charles said laughingly. "Flap those wings! Soar like a 14-year-old, bruised-bottomed butterfly!"

"I'm hungry," abruptly Hector said. "Let's eat." Into the house the three boys went. Once inside, Charles reminded them that their parents were still sleeping, so they needed to be quiet. Hector and William began to act like stealth ninjas chopping imaginary enemies while tip-toeing into the kitchen and then using a spoon as their ninja swords.

They each poured themselves a bowl of cereal and Charles said, in a whisper, "Let's bless this mess." William and Hector bowed their heads. "Good morning, God," Charles began, "We want to thank you for our guy time, bonding in our tent and having fun spanking William." Hector and William laughed as William pushed Hector's chair with his foot under the table, nearly sending Hector to the floor.

"Sshhh!" Charles said to the boys as he continued his prayer. "We thank you for this wonderful smorg-us-borg placed before us, and we pray that William can really enjoy his birthday today. We pray God that you would make clear to William the meaning and purpose behind this ability to see white and dark angels. We pray that we could all want to know you more and seek your face. Amen."

"Amen," William said. Hector simply nodded his head and began to eat his cereal. Suddenly, Hector sprang from his seat, ran out of the room, and left the other two puzzled as to what was going on. They heard a drawer open and then shut. Hector ran back to William with a candle and a small box of matches.

"What are you doing?" Charles asked.

"Just wait," Hector answered. Hector stuck a candle into William's cereal and lit the candle with a match and then began to sing "Happy Birthday" in a whisper as William laughed and said, "Hurry up! My cereal is getting soggy!" Charles began to sing as well. William went to blow out the candle, but knocked the flame into the milk. They all laughed in hushed voices.

After the messy breakfast and a quick tent breakdown and cleanup from the raccoon invasion of the trash, Charles dropped William off at his house.

William's dad was walking to his car to leave for work when Charles arrived at William's house. "Happy birthday, William!" his dad exclaimed from across the yard, still making his way to his vehicle as William got out of Charles's old truck. His mom peeped through the window, ran out the door, grabbed William, and hugged him, saying, "Happy birthday, honey!"

The wonderful music of his mother's angel spoke: *"I feel a lightened heart awakening inside, let go of the hold of darkness and be new in Christ; accept Grace."* William's angel swooped to the side of him and raged back. *"Insults you give, not gifts that I have for him to delight . . . Dark he is, dark he will stay."*

William was getting tired of this warfare.

"You, um, got some marshmallow on your face." She licked her thumb and was making her way to clean up the mellow mess, but William intercepted the classic motherly move by using his own spit on the palm of his hand to remove the crystallized sugar.

"I will be home early. Happy birthday!" his dad hollered from his rolled-down window while pulling out of the driveway.

"Thanks, Dad," William responded in a smile. William and his mom walked inside the house as William did a last big wave and shouted "Thanks!" to Charles.

His mom asked, "So, what do you want to do today?"

"I'm kinda tired. I didn't get much sleep last night and I smell like a bonfire. Do you think I could just shower and sleep?" William asked.

"Sure," his mom responded. "Did you have fun last night?"

"Yeah, it was a blast! Hector's mom made chicken pot pie and homemade blackberry pie for dinner and it was pie-rific!" William said, with a pool of saliva forming at his lips.

"What would you like for breakfast?" his mom asked.

"Oh, I already . . . "William stopped short of finishing his statement to allow his eager mother to give her son special attention on his birthday.

"I could make waffles?" she said. William replied, "That sounds great, as he headed off to shower.

When William returned to the kitchen, his mom had waffles and a glass of milk ready for the both of them. Sitting across from his mother at the table, William asked, "Mom, how do you know if you are going to Heaven?"

She did not seem bothered by the direct question. "Well," she began, "going to Heaven is the result of believing that Jesus is the perfect Son of God."

"Charles said that even demons believe God exists, but demons cannot go to Heaven."

"Yes, Charles is correct. Demons do exist and they do believe that God is real, but only believing that God is real is not enough to go to Heaven. In order to go to Heaven you have to believe that God exists, that Jesus is God's perfect Son, and enter into a relationship with Jesus. You are saved from your sin by Jesus only, not by your own good works."

William was eager to know more. His angel was not so eager for William to learn truth—and began whistling out of tune.

"What do you mean by good works?"

"Well, we as Christ-followers are called to do good deeds, but not that we may earn our way to Heaven, but out of gratitude for the gift of eternal life in Heaven," his mother, well-versed in the Scriptures, said. "We all have sinned and fall short of the glory of God, but we can rejoice knowing that Jesus did overcome the world, choosing to live, die, and save his people, if they choose to accept Him. Being saved is not just a prayer and then doing whatever each sees fitting; but it's a daily walk with Jesus, growing in knowledge and living out actions of love. To run in the footsteps of our Creator, doing our best to imitate the actions of Jesus, through prayer, reading your Bible, and being in community with other believers."

William sat across from her with a half-waffle suspended on his fork and the other half dangling from his teeth, awestruck at the new information download. William took the bite left on his fork and paused from his waffle devouring to notice the whistling had stopped and his angel was shaking, hunkering down on the floor beside him. William liked the sight of his creepy stalker feeling ill!

In much need of answers, William dared to ask, "So how do I get a light angel?" The once-calm mother now paused and inhaled strongly as the voices and images of the night they had shared dinner with Mr. Wiker replayed in her head. The prayer spoken by her own son about dark and light angels resounded louder in her ears than she remembered; did William actually believe that he could see angels? Did he ask about white angels because he himself had a dark angel? William shifted in his seat, playing relaxed, eating his last few morsels of soggy waffle with delight, oblivious to the uneasiness his mother felt over this most recent question.

Her heart rate was racing and the sweat formed on her palms rapidly as she spoke once more on the most important decision one could ever make. "William, I am not really sure what you mean of how you get a white angel, but I do know that darkness cannot remain when light is present; so to get rid of the darkness, one must bring the light. Jesus is that light, and with him in your heart, darkness will have nowhere to hide."

She gazed above her only son's head to try and capture some image of what he may be seeing, but only found an uncombed mess of hair sitting on a beautiful sun-soaked head of a boy searching for answers she didn't have.

## CHAPTER TWENTY-FOUR

# Busted Balloons

*R*ING... RING. The classic melody of the kitchen telephone broke the serious silence once more. The phone William and Hector seemed to make fun of on a regular basis was becoming more of a serious emotional relief machine, taking the pressure away from words unsaid and forcing normalcy to surface again. William stayed at the table as his mom strolled to pick up the phone. With an overly cheerful greeting, she answered, "Hello!"

"Sue, Hi, yes, doing well... ummm ummmm..." She paused. "He did..." William's eyes bugged out; he had not thought of the consequences his little switch of the birthday cards at the party would bring. William stood quickly to drop his plate off in the sink so he could hide in his room. But he was not quick enough and was captured like a fly in a flytrap. "Oh wait, William is just right here," his mom spoke causally, all the while frantically motioning with her hand as she mouthed "get over here!" With her well-polished glossy finger nails clutching the phone, she drummed her toe impatiently, waiting for William to take the handset. William tried shaking his head No! to avoid talking to his aunt on the phone, but Mom had the death stare, and there was no escape.

Before a minute passed, William held the phone, awaiting the familiar squeaky voice to ring clear. Despite the frown embedded on his face, he tried to carry a smile in his voice to lessen the shame he felt. Then Aunt Sue chirped her intent: "Hi there, sweetie. Just wanted to give you a call and thank you for the four-piece toaster set." Aunt Sue spoke a bit too enthusiastically.

"Yeah," William said with a guilty exhale. William scratched his head and stared around the room, unable to come to terms with speaking the truth. "You must have been saving your allowance for months. It was just so sweet of you, Willy Billy." His aunt continued with her praise.

"Uh huh," William said, gritting his teeth, still wrestling to speak truth as he attempted to end the conversation and his guilt. Aunt Sue—occupied with hearing herself speak—continued on. "Oh, sonny boy, also a big happy birthday to you! Twelve is such a grown-up age." William, unwilling to add time to the conversation, now chose to agree instead of argue, and decided to not mention his actual age of 14.

"Yup, it sure is." William said, doing his best to sound engaged.

"Well, I best be off, my cat is caught in a coat. Bye now!" Aunt Sue said suddenly.

William, standing against the wall, exhaled in relief, realizing he had escaped admitting his wrongdoing. "Bye," William said, confused from hearing such nonsensical remarks of farewell. Although William thought he was perhaps out of trouble with his Aunt Sue, he failed to remember that both his mother and father may yet discover what he had done and discipline him accordingly.

As William turned to leave the kitchen, his mother asked, "What was that all about?" In a laid-back response he answered, "Oh, she just wanted to thank me for the card I made for her birthday." William had provided his best, terrible lying voice, unaware of his mother's insight on the situation.

"Really? . . . Aunt Sue said you got her a four-piece toaster set?" William's mother now said, bringing her hands to her hips in disappointment. It was *the look;* he often received a similar look from his father—it was all that was needed to strike fear into his being so that he would not repeat the offense. William swallowed strongly, as if a peach had been logged in his throat. His mother, in a deeper, serious tone, spoke without blinking her eyes. "Why is Aunt Sue thanking you for a toaster set that sweet little old lady Robin bought, with my help?"

William stuttered with his mother's words in his ears, filling like a worm on the pavement in July. "I . . . I . . . OK, I am sorry," William said forcefully, not exactly heartfelt. William felt more frustrated at being called out rather than ashamed at his wrongful decision.

"You have some apologizing to do, mister, starting with your Aunt Sue," William's mother said with a pointed finger at the phone.

"Awwww, Mom, do I have to? Can't you just tell her?"

"William Edger Jones, you made this mess and you are going to clean it up." She spoke firmly; use of the full name meant she was all business.

She quickly scribbled down the two numbers for Sue and Mrs. Robin, then handed William the receiver. "Birthday boy or not . . . you make this right."

## CHAPTER TWENTY-FIVE

# Say It Again

*Flash forward . . .*

12:04      William grudgingly dials his aunt, hoping to receive the answering machine, but to his dismay, a bubbly Aunt Sue picks up the line.

12:12      Finishing explaining and his apology, Aunt Sue is still jabbering with her bubbly tone and saying she knew the whole time. Unfortunately, she failed to understand the fact William is 14 not 12, although William had already shared this piece of information twice.

12:18      Another phone call, with old lady Robin picking up the phone. William yells the whole apology because of her bad hearing.

# HICCUP EFFECT

| | |
|---|---|
| 12:28 | William repeats the entire apology, yelling and in a slow motion-type-of-speaking voice, because old lady Robin forgot to turn on her hearing aid. |
| 12:35 | After saying good-bye four times, William hangs up phone, wipes his brow, and exhales strongly. |
| 1:00 | Mother asks William to decorate dining room with streamers and balloons. |
| 1:15 | William is red-faced from blowing up balloons, blacks out on his back. |
| 1:18 | Wakes up and finishes five more balloons. Looks around and frown sat not having more balloons. |
| 1:22 | Decides to try streamer decorating instead. |
| 1:36 | Realizes once more that decorating is not his thing now that the doorframe displays torn blue and green paper—more of a mess than a masterpiece. |
| 2:35 | Buzzer sounds from the oven. |
| 2:41 | Sweet birthday cake aroma floats into the awfully garnished balloon-and-paper-littered dining room. |
| 3:00 | William's dad enters the house giving hellos and hugs; both man and boy attempt to snitch some of the freshly baked cake. Dark angel's high-five too; they like to be in company with their own kind. |
| 3:02 | Unsuccessful attempt to "thief" some cake and more decorating continues. This time with much more victory, as William's dad and his large lung capacity takes over the balloon inflating, filling up ten balloons in ten minutes as opposed to William's five in fifteen minutes. |

| | |
|---|---|
| 3:32 | Father finishes the remaining bag of balloons to reveal a sea of blue inflated waves although, to William, it is boring grays and darker grays. The streamers swaying in the natural air of the windows being open produce an immediate party environment, despite the ever-creepy shadows of swords and demons. For now, in William's world, that deep thinking would have to wait. |
| 4:00 | One man and one teen instructed to take showers, for the guests would be arriving in an hour and a half. |
| 4:08 | William burnt temporarily from the water in the shower; someone must be using the washer, he thinks. |
| 4:12 | William, fully in his birthday suit, soap in hair, eyes closed, tiptoes to the door, cracks it open, and yells, "Turn off the washer!" "Oops" and "Sorry" are called up in return from downstairs. |
| 4:14 | William on his back (slipping on the wet floor) flips himself over onto the fuzzy yellow rug. He crawls to his feet with blinded, soapy eyes, desperate for the power of clean water. |
| 4:20 | Now back in the shower, eyes no longer burning, and hair free from shampoo, he reaches for the lavender bar of soap, pretending he didn't care that it smelled like his grandma. But, as is normal for William, the bar of soap flies out of his pruned, wrinkled palms and over the shower curtain. |
| 4:21 | William pulls back the shower curtain, eyes zoom in on the lavender grandma-smelling bar of soap—now floating in the toilet. |
| 4:22 | Shrugs his shoulders and finishes his shower. It would be a lavender surprise for the next visitor |

| | |
|---|---|
| | to the toilet. |
| 4:32 | Wraps the towel like a fruit basket on his head, walks past the mirror, and says BOO! to the angel smoothing his own oily locks back. Angel just gives him a wink of his dark eyes and says, *"It's just you and me buddy. And what a pair to see."* |
| 5:00 | Dressed and playing with plastic figurines under the bed. Finding childhood activities calm his nerves. Although if he got too nervous, William would just yawn uncontrollably. |
| 5:06 | Running down the stairs, jumps the last four steps and crashes to his knees, attempting to tuck and roll. Looks more like a fish out of water. |
| 5:28 | First guests arrive, all family, hugs, lipstick-staining kisses, cheek-face-squeezing, happy birthday wishes given and thank you's spoken. A frenzy of voices came in and out of William's ears from both dark and light angels. It becomes apparent that many relatives' angels were what he expected. The alcoholic uncle that always seemed to be yelling at reunions was being followed by a vicious knife-carrying thug of an angel-demon dressed in rugged leather cut-off pants. Whereas his perfectly put together cousin who always was considerate of others' needs was being followed by an angel lovely in appearance carrying a javelin, and not afraid to use it if darkness tried to creep in. The battle was always at hand if Christ's name was said. He was seeing a pattern of fighting and persuading between the opposing sides. |
| 7:00 | "AHHH!" is heard from the upstairs bathroom. |

|       |                                                                                                                                                                                                                                                                                                                               |
| ----- | ------------------------------------------------------------------------------------------------------------------------------------------------------------------------------------------------------------------------------------------------------------------------------------------------------------------------------ |
|       | … "Why is my Christmas soap I gave Helen in the toilet?" called a surprised and grumpy Aunt Marge. William hides on the sun porch to avoid being questioned.                                                                                                                                                                 |
| 7:09  | William's smile is fading, belly happy with cake, ugly sweater given and forced to wear by parents, all to show appreciation of Great Grandma Eugene, who was so blind she would not have noticed if a camel showed up at the party.                                                                                         |
| 7:11  | William wants to drown himself in the punch bowl out of embarrassing baby stories being shared by all, especially the one involving him attempting to run from home with his knapsack holding only a potato and a pair of whitey tighties. "Boy, was he prepared," William heard his father chime in.                        |
| 7:30  | William somehow manages to slip away upstairs and packs his bags with little form of organization for camp, using the wad-and-stuff method.                                                                                                                                                                                  |
| 7:35  | Bag zipped up. "All done."                                                                                                                                                                                                                                                                                                   |
| 7:37  | Forgot what he actually packed into his bag and dumps all the contents onto the floor and chooses to follow the list provided to him by camp.                                                                                                                                                                                |
| 8:02  | Forced to give hugs to all who attended the birthday party for him, although it seemed more like a mom-and-dad chitchat party than a birthday for William. The voices give him advice either helpful or hateful, depending on the angel that followed each face.                                                             |
| 8:30  | Mom, Dad, and William now walk around the house cleaning up a mess of cups, napkins, and wrapping paper. The balloons and streamers                                                                                                                                                                                          |

| | could stay for another day. |
|---|---|
| 9:00 | In bed, teeth brushed, good-nights shared. William feels cozy and falls into a deep sleep until a poke in his side wakes him swiftly. |

William rolled off the sheets, exposing a lump under the covers that must have jabbed his side. The sheet was hiding a small gift wrapped in a white cloth, the color that stood out to his eyes the most. A color he wanted to see more of above his head. He carefully unwrapped the container to reveal a genuine, hide-leather-bound journal. He flipped the pages; they were mostly filled. He opened the front inscription, more scribbled than written, and read: "A thought of mine to share to yours of how to be less of me. DAD."

William hugged it to his chest and prayed, and when he said "Jesus" the angel that haunted his day and night melted like fog in the morning's glow. *How long would it stay away? . . .* he thought. He hoped forever.

## CHAPTER TWENTY-SIX

# Worn Pages

"T-minus 25 minutes till pick-up time," William said out loud as he threw off his bed sheets. He grabbed his bags and walked downstairs, dropping them at the front door. His dad yelled from the kitchen: "Morning, William."

"Mornin' to you," responded William as he grabbed some cereal.

"All packed and ready for camp?" he said to his son, who was busy eating.

"Yeah, Charles should be here soon," William responded. "Where's mom?" he said with a mouthful of cereal.

"She is in the backyard. Did you have fun yesterday? You sure got allot of presents," his dad said, making small talk.

"Yeah, it was a lot of fun," William replied, continuing to chow down on his breakfast.

Now in a more serious tone of voice, William's dad stated, "So, your mom told me about the 'present' you gave to your Aunt Sue."

There was a long, silent pause, then in a blurt William answered: "I am sorry. I really learned my lesson." William was sitting upright with his best posture, but his eyes were not settling.

His dad now spoke calmly. "William, this isn't about learning your lesson, but rather of doing what is right and not doing what is wrong."

To William, it still seemed the same. "But isn't that a lesson?" William answered, a bit smart-alecky. His father sat without words or expression; William was quickly getting the picture.

William's father did not feel like he was much of a teacher to his one and only son. Sure, he taught William how to ride a bike, throw a ball, and tell a joke. But a *deep* teacher? William's father was realizing that he had missed out on too many opportunities in order to be the first to teach his own son many of life's lessons. Those life-lesson learning moments had been filled by his wife or William's teachers from school or even William's friends. William's father recognized now how often he let teachable moments slip by, and it saddened him greatly. It seemed like a wave of insight had overpowered him in which he realized that his son was truly becoming a young man, understanding right and wrong, learning how to choose his friends, and for the most part, obeying his parents.

William, realizing his dad was thinking serious thoughts and wanting to avoid the punishment his dad was conjuring up, quickly left the table to finish getting ready. "Is he here?" William's dad asked, seeing William walking out of the kitchen.

"No, he'll be here in five minutes," William said, heading off to brush his teeth. There was a short pause, and then William's dad met him at the front door.

"So, did you find the secret surprise in your sheets?" his dad asked, crossing his arms in the hope that William liked it.

"That was my journal that I had received when I was about your age from my father. I have filled most of those pages with my thoughts about a life of joys and failure. I want you to learn from my mistakes and avoid having to make them yourself. William, it's yours now. I want you to read it and write your thoughts in it. And when you get older, you can give it to your son. . . . If you want." William's dad said all this as if it were a well-rehearsed speech.

"Cool," was all William said as he reached for and embraced his dad. "Thanks, Dad." The hug was not long, but the voice of another form of darkness that hung above his father said: *"You are growing more and more like your father. William, don't change who you are."* William pulled back quickly, trying to wipe out the unwelcoming voice of his dad's demon-angel from his head. William smiled again as he placed the treasured journal into his bag. Worn and crumbling binding made packing it in William's stuffed back pack a challenge to not break such a prized possession. . . well, at least not in front of his dad.

## CHAPTER TWENTY-SEVEN

# Name Calling

William threw his bag into the bed of the truck and jumped into the cab. "Mornin', Sunshine," Charles said with a little too much energy.

"Hey, guys," William said in return. William waved out the window as the vehicle pulled away from the house. The boys traveled all snug in the truck with little cares of the road.

"You get any cool gifts for your birthday?" asked Hector, being Mr. Nosey.

"Not really," William answered. "Mostly money in cards, a weird sweater, and someone got me plastic containers for my lunch!"

"What?" Charles asked. "Plastic containers?"

"When did you become a pregnant mom?" Hector said, poking fun.

"I know, right?" William agreed. "I set up the containers in my room as a drum set," said William, "but then my mom took them away and put them in the kitchen."

Hector and Charles laughed at the image of William having a musical solo on a plastic, makeshift drum set.

Hector turned serious. "So we're going to pick up Penny, but since there is no more space, you're going to have to sit in the back and she will sit up here next to me."

"Whatever," William said, shoving his shoulder into Hector's.

"Yeah, I might have even put my arm around her," Hector said as he demonstrated his casual yawn-and-reach technique to put his arm over William's shoulder. A voice broke the humor and spoke to William in a whisper: *"Look at your friendship and how close you two are. Never change, William."* William remained calm and just playfully laughed, to avoid a scene.

"Get off, Hector," William said, pushing him away.

The truck was bumping along the road from well-worn potholes that never seemed to get fixed when an oncoming bus began to cross the line into their lane. "Watch out!" shouted Hector, who was riding in the middle.

William silently watched as his dark angel swooped in front of the truck with his sword and a dramatic *Pop!* The wheel must have been sliced to burst. Charles was losing control of the steering and overcorrected his turning, sending the tail swerving from side to side. The bus horn blared as if that would help Charles' driving skills. The bus veered forcefully across the lane; William saw another angel swoop in front of the truck—Charles' glowing light angel pushed the bus further past his truck. The truck front passenger light nicked the back bumper of the school bus and sent the worn-out truck spinning. William could hear his angel laughing and cheering for them to crash. The bus came to a halt along the wrong side of the road and the driver hurried to check all his child passengers on board. The truck finally stopped whirling around and settled on the grassy median along the road. The truck light was not even busted or cracked and the bus and its campers were all well and safe. All three boys in the classic green truck rested their heads against the back seat rest and blankly stared out the window, sighing deeply at having avoiding death-by-bus, at least for now.

Hector, who had been planning what funny comments to make about William and Penny all morning was now just glad to be alive. So he stopped picking on William and sat quietly for once.

Forty minutes later, after the police had promptly responded to and recorded the details of the near crash, the boys arrived at camp. The sign read "Happy Howard Ranch, established 1983." They drove down the lane shaded by trees and passed wooden cabins marked clearly by number and name. But as they drove closer, they realized that each cabin was renamed with painted cardboard signs tied in a makeshift way on the porch railings. They read them as they traveled to the head cabin for check-in. "Cabin # 4 MALE MEN." *A bit cheesy,* the boys thought, but they read on. "Cabin #7 DAMSELS WITHOUT DISTRESS." "Cabin #2 WOOF ARTED."

All the boys in the rough-riding truck laughed at that one. Charles pulled into the rock-lined dirt parking space. Each boy jumped out of the truck and headed to the many tables lined up for registration. They received their assigned cabins; William and Hector had been placed in the same one. "Cabin #6 SHADOW HAWK." But when they arrived at their cabin, the new recycle-friendly sign read, "CHEST HAIR." Hector and William stood, puzzled. William interrupted their pondering. "Chest hair . . . I don't have any chest hair . . . I want some, but so far I just have this awkward patch in the middle of my belly button. Puberty is not so nice sometimes."

"Oh, come on . . . it's manly," Hector said, attempting to flex his non-visible muscles. "Who is our cabin leader?"

"It says Robert Catner," William said.

"Aww, man, I want to be in your cabin, Charles," said Hector, with whininess in his voice.

Charles seemed surprised at his little brother's comment. "What? I thought you wanted to be in someone else's cabin?" Charles said, remembering the conversation he had with his brother earlier.

"Can't you see if we can switch to your cabin?" Hector requested. "Just tell them I am allergic to cats. . . . Cuz his name is CAT-ner." Hector chuckled at his own joke.

William tried to chime in, adding, "Yeah, and tell them I am allergic to 'Ners.'" Hector laughed at the lame add-on, rather than William's wit.

Charles, delighted at the two boys' requests, said, "I'll see what I can do." The two boys chatted to themselves, watching the cars bring in the happy campers and those who were walking to their cabins. They stood there waiting for Charles to return. Then William's jaw dropped as he looked upon the loveliest face he had ever seen in all 14 years of being alive. . . . that of Penny's. It seemed odd that a boy would respond so awestruck each time he saw her, as if it were the first time to lay eyes on her. William attempted to wave, but his staring got the best of his hand-waving speed, and he missed his chance to see if she waved back.

"What was that all about?" Hector said. "You turn into such a dweeb when she is around."

William agreed with Hector by nodding his agreement as Charles walked back with the news. "You are officially switched to cabin #8 HAZELNUT!" Charles said in his most professional voice.

"Yeah!!" each boy cheered.

"So what is our new cabin name called?" William asked.

"No, that is the changed name; it used to be 'Pine Cone.'" Charles said. He did not understand the lack of coolness in the name Hazelnut.

"What kind of creativeness is that, changing one nature item for the next?" Hector blurted out, "It sounds like a girly candle! What happened to the super-manly names like WOOF ARTED and CHEST HAIR? We might as well just call it cabin #8." Hector's excitement kept draining from his face as his brother claimed his cabin didn't have such a sissy title.

"I like hazelnuts," William said, fully content with the name of his new cabin.

"Yeah, well, we should just change the name to 'The Cabin That Smells like Girly Candles!'" Hector spoke again, rolling his eyes.

"We're keeping the name, Hazelnut," Charles said in defense, "Because I like it."

The conversation ended on the matter of naming the cabin and the boys gathered their bags and headed toward the new cabin a few buildings away. They arrived at their new humble abode. They walked up to the porch and opened the aged-wooden door. The aroma of cedar, smelly socks, and mothballs filled their noses. It was perfect.

And the days at Happy Howard Ranch seemed to fly by in a flash.

## CHAPTER TWENTY-EIGHT

# Wednesday

Charles and his Hazelnut kids introduced themselves, picked out their bunks, and made up secret handshakes. Canteen Dinner was at 6 p.m. in the main building, renamed by the campers as "SEE FOOD." The first night the camp director came and spoke in front of the many campers. He was called Chief Howard, or Ranger Howard, depending on his dress for the day. This evening he was Chief Howard, and he bounced into the dining hall with feathered hat and face painted, humming some offbeat "Ah E Ha, Ah E Ha, Ah E Ha." He used over-exaggerated hand gestures and tiptoed around in his moccasins.

He gave the story of the camp and how it began—likely two minutes of truth and ten minutes of "creative" details involving wolves and lions and any other manly words that make a good story great. After the meal, each cabin was given freedom to roam the grounds and become acquainted with the camp and other campers. William and Hector found the bunk next to the window to be less sunken in than the others.

They spent the next few hours trying to casually bump into Penny and her friends. They managed to bump into campers from the "Chest Hair" cabin and decided it would be best to avoid them on all occasions. William alone had the understanding that all the boys in that cabin had dark angel punks to help out with their all-too-prevalent mischief. The terror in the eyes of the boys was enough to scare the hair out of your ears, so William made sure to not make contact with any of the Chest Hair dudes. He was not about to find out what their demon buddies wanted to say. This, despite the fact his angel kept finding ways to guide him to get closer to those mean teens.

## CHAPTER TWENTY-NINE

# Thursday

Wake up came at 6:45 to the sound of Charles attempting to yodel—an extremely loud solo. "Mile high" pancakes are served for canteen breakfast. One of the kids burps the entire alphabet into the microphone—extremely impressive, William and Hector agreed. Canoe trip on the lake; William tips canoe and Hector falls out. Hector tips canoe, and William falls out. Charles tips canoe, William and Hector both fall out.

Lunch time: man in banana suit runs through canteen followed by another man in a gorilla suit. Banana-suited man keeps shouting "I am banana!" Banana suit gets tripped by the untitled leader of the Chest Hair cabin. He had himself, one might say, a real banana split.

After their full stomachs digested turkey sandwiches, it was zip line time through the woods. William screams like little sissy girl; does not want to go again. Hector makes fun of William by screaming like a sissy girl; also decides he does not want to go again. Then free swim time at the lake and William sees Penny for the second time since camp began. He wants to go and talk with her, but he is on the inflatable balloon on the lake about to be blobbed by the biggest kid at camp. William is not even sure this boy is a camper, seeing his size and all. William turns to tell the camper he no longer wants to be blobbed, but it is too late—the extremely large kid is already airborne and hurtling downward toward him. William is launched into the air—a view he could have done without—and pounds into the lake's surface, the water feeling more like a brick than warm lake water. William's skin is transformed from a soft pink tan into a lobster red. William spends a good five minutes trying to recover from his airborne flight experience by wallowing on the sandy banks on his back. Penny skips by: "Saw your swan dive . . . really impressive."

"Yeah, thanks," groaned William, in plenty of pain.

Dinner canteen arrives soon after lake clean up. The main course for the night is double sloppy Moe's. Each cabin performs a skit. The "Male Men" take newspaper and throw it at the crowd, yelling "Papers, Papers!" in a half-recognizable New York accent. No one laughs; their cabin leader is the only one to clap. Then "Woof Arted" found the stage and a microphone and made farting sounds for five minutes. All kids under 15 laughs out loud for their entire performance. Adults look away, hoping to hinder the laughter and hide their own personal amusement at the fart solos.

Then it was the girls' cabins' time to prove themselves. "Damsels Not In Distress" was up first, doing a cheerleading chant that spelled out their cabin's name. Some laughed out of embarrassment for them, but not for their creativity. Then the group that William would have voted as winner even if they had not performed was up next: "Unipegicornisus," Penny's cabin.

They discovered later that the name was a combination of a Unicorn and a Pegasus. Too bad it is not a real animal, William and Hector thought, because having a horn and wings would just be awesome. The eclectic array of girls entered the stage with sleeping bags on their waists and cardboard wings on their backs. Each girl took a turn at opera singing—which, truthfully, was a skill they had not yet gained. The audience shoved fingers in eardrums to withstand the unpleasant display of what these campers thought to be music.

Meanwhile, the dark angel above Penny was holding her bow at ready. *Who was she at war with?; Penny is just singing,* William thought. There was a girl next to Penny whose angel kept whirling rocks from a sling toward Penny's darkness, but the darkness kept ducking down to avoid any collision. The bow remained aimed and ready, but no shots were taken. Her dark angel knees were buckling as if a heavy weight was upon her wings. *How could she be so wonderfully nice to everyone and have a flipping dark angel? . . . What is the deal?* William thought.

One fellow camper in the crowd didn't mind the screeches of disdained "harmony"—he gave applause aplenty . . . It was William who stood up and clapped alone, whistling and cheering until Hector yanked his arm to sit down. The jerk on his arm sent a jerk to his ears, giving voice again to the dagger-holding lightless winged man beside Hector: *"Your dream girl awaits, your hearts are already alike, be her all by staying true to you."* William forced his hand away and yelled "No!" wishing he had just thought his yelling instead. "Woa, easy, just sit down before you make a fool out of me," Hector said in a whisper to William.

Next the "Hazelnut" cabin jumps up for its moment to shine. Charles is dressed like a hazelnut, although his costume is made from a crumpled old fridge box, making him appear as either a rock or a brown potato. The kids in the cabin have baseball bats shaped from cardboard and begin beating the hazelnut, with Charles inside, like a piñata for several minutes. Charles flops onto the ground and Hector ends the "skit" with the only words spoken: "Hey, where is all the candy?" No one laughs, though "Woof Arted" responded with more farting sounds from the back of the room.

The night did not end there, though. A campfire full-out with roasted marshmallows, chocolate, and not-so-scary stories captured the rest of the evening. Sleep found most of the campers not too long after their sugar comas came crashing down. All except those who had over-imaginative minds and let the not-scary stories none the less turn into a fear of bunnies stealing their socks in the night.

## CHAPTER THIRTY

# Friday

Another early rise, at 6:45, for cabin #8. Charles is shouting a terrible rap song on the roof of the cabin. "Hamburger, hamburger . . . in a bun . . . don't you know . . . I like to run . . . Hamburger Hamburger . . . Better wake up . . . or it's water on your head . . . from a cup . . . "

The campers rolled over with a little energy after hearing that water would be poured on their heads if they didn't get moving.

Breakfast turns into a must-be-brave time for William as he finds himself sitting next to Penny. He actually can't remember if he sat next to her or her next to him. Either way, he was thrilled and found himself actually able to hold a conversation with her. It may have consisted of the food items on his plate, and the results of the food he ate last night. But Penny didn't go running, so he figured he was doing all right. Hector added to the conversation by crawling under the table and making fart sounds, attempting to embarrass William, but it had not been the best of imitations and, truthfully, sounded more like a dehydrated elephant trumpeting spit sounds.

Penny leaned over and rested her head on William. He held extremely still, hoping to not scare away this delicate butterfly. The voice of the Hawaiian haunting darkness came rhythmically into his ears. *"Dance with me, sing to me, I will be, all you need . . . You are all you need to seek, stop these questions of darkness for light, and hold the hand next to you strong and tight."* William wanted to hold Penny's hand for as long as he had known her name, but now, with the gorgeous demon suggesting it, he felt the darkness hot and uninviting. So he simply slid away, out of reach of her enchanting spell.

The day rolled on with a group mud fight by the lake. *Goggles never looked so good on a girl,* William thought as he looked at Penny from across the pit of gooey mess. William's trance was interrupted by a flying mud missile that thumped into his chest. The object of the game was to capture the flag of the opposing color's team; unlucky as it was for William, he could not decipher which color flag was his. His team lost in soccer due to his inability to remember which goal was his and now his team won due to him capturing his own flag and letting the other team slip and slide around trying to recapture it. "Nice strategy, holding the flag hostage . . . classic move, man," said Joe, one of William's mud-covered teammates.

"Well, I am all about strategy," William lied.

"Oh, and you got some mud in your braces . . . you might want to get that out," William shared to another, probably a bit too forward, especially since the camper had come to congratulate him for his well-planned maneuver.

Fun in the sun ended with crusted mud on faces and hair; the rest of the morning was free time to clean up until lunch. Lunch arrived as a picnic on the porch. The meal was even visited by some unlucky dude in a Clown-Bear costume. The costumed dude waved and made hand gestures but didn't say a word. But the angel that lingered above the bear was beautiful and white, with glowing long hair—and it was no dude at all. The form was graceful and elegant, nothing like the suit that hid the lady inside. William was starting to see the benefits of this capability of his. He would have automatically judged the suit to be a "dude." He felt a lift to his spirit, of care for those around him, to judge not by outward appearance, but to find the beauty within.

The meal was rushed to a finish when the bear handed out a map of the campground; it contained marked-out locations with clues that led to a mysterious treasure. All the campers were off on the adventure. The most important rule of the woods was to "never roam alone." William and Hector proposed a crafty plan. During all the running around of the scavenger hunt, the "Hazelnutters" could sneak into the "Unipegacornisus" cabin and tee-pee their bunks.

Unfortunately, they shared their plan to the other Nutters a bit too loudly and "Woof Arted" and "Chest Hair" overheard their plans. When the Nutters arrived at the girl's cabin ready for the attack of the toilet paper, they failed to notice the door was already open. As they crept closer and were about to slip inside, they were overcome by squirt guns from the Woofers and Chest Hair dudes, sending the other boys running. "Woof Arted" did a victory trumpet sound of farting and "Chest Hair" beat their chests wildly at seeing their enemy flee.

The Hazelnutters ran with haste at their defeat, attempting to get the soggy toilet paper off their hands and shoes. William and Hector set out to solve the treasure map, but only made it to the second clue when the main cabin bell rang. "Male Men" had won the treasure. A basket of snacks and red handkerchiefs was the prize, which they proudly wore on their heads the remaining time at camp. The boys still in the darkness of the woods walked back, defeated, to the main cabin.

They were a mere twenty yards from exiting the foliage when a ferocious growl poured forth from the shadowed woods.

The teens' feet froze in fear. They turned to face the threat. A twig crunched in their direction. William and Hector screamed instinctively. They found each other in a most awkward side hug; waiting whatever it was that was going to reveal itself. A voice from above Hector spoke out to William.

*"You're safe in the darkness."*

"Don't let me die!" Hector blurted out.

"What was that!?!" shouted William as the growl came again, sounding close enough to touch. The boys didn't stay around to find out. They sprinted for the cabins and for sunlight. They arrived out of breath, where the cabin leader of the "Male Men" was being given the cabin's grand prize. William and Hector received many looks for their interruptive entrance. Another counselor standing near the back leaned over and said, "What happened to you guys?" Before Hector could respond to the question, a deeper and louder growl penetrated the ears of all who were standing there.

Many screams exited from the smaller campers. All were waiting to see what thing had bellowed such a haunting sound. William thought it was incredibly stupid to simply wait—shouldn't they be running away or taking shelter? Yet, he remained still himself. The growl was a stone's throw away and came once again. Penny, unknown to William was standing right beside him, grabbed his hand in her sudden fright . . . William, in slow realization, looked at his hand interlaced with Penny's, and then at her eyes.

"It will be ALL RGHT!" William shouted, rather than whispering, as he was startled by another growl. The dark angel from above Penny gave this statement to William: *"Is it not fate the two of you, same are your hearts. This is who you are."* William, frustrated at the unwelcoming voice, but too overjoyed to release her hand, remained motionless.

And then . . . out of the covering of the trees stepped the familiar voice of Ranger Howard. "Howdy, partners!" It had been him all along, making his bobcat call in the woods. For William, it was worth being freaked out of his socks, because he was holding the hand of a rare beauty. He continued to hold Penny's dainty hand as if fear still gripped her. William must not have realized his grip was too strong, since he found that Penny was producing a painful face.

"Can I . . . have my hand back?" Penny said with softness in her voice.

William, embarrassed from holding her hand too tightly, quickly shoved his hands into his pockets and began whistling a random tune.

The counselors organized their groups and announced that it was time to head to their assigned cabins—with the emphasis on "assigned"—and that lights would be out in ten minutes. No girls in boys' cabins, or boys in girls' cabins. Penny bumped into William's shoulder with a big smile. "Bye," she simply said.

"Yeah, bye . . . nice not getting eaten by bobcats with you," William said with a wave. Penny grabbed the nearest girl friend to skip away with. Hector, who had witnessed the entire scene, came over and patted William on the back.

"Well done, man, acted like a real pro." William would have relaxed and agreed, but the dark stalker jumped in the conversation too. *"Friend so true, so find what you want and get it with all desires met, Penny is yours, and Hector will help you."*

William coughed and stepped out of contact with the dark angel.

"For a second, I thought you actually knew what you were doing. You know, positioning yourself close to Penny, keeping your palm open and available, but then you blurted out 'ALL RIGHT!'" Hector said. "Then I realized you were flying by the seat of your pants the whole thing. Regardless, I think you did awesome."

"Thanks, man," William said, beginning to blush. Hector quickly slapped William's rear end and ran off, shouting as he ran. "Last one to brush their teeth sleeps on the bottom bunk!" Which neither wanted to do, for it contained more pee stains on it than could be counted. They both raced to the line of teenage boys eagerly awaiting their turns at the faucet outside their cabin.

William was able to beat Hector at his own game and claimed the top bunk as his trophy. They came into the cabin and each boy was focused on their individual nighttime routine. For some boys, it only required a tiny fluffing of their pillows, while others needed blankets up to their chins, and still others just flopped onto their beds with their shoes still on. William noticed in the corner of the room that Charles was talking with a boy who had his head lowered. Charles' hand was on the boy's shoulder.

William could see the battle raging on above the two quiet boys. Charles's angel—brighter white than normal—had a drawn sword and was fighting with full gusto against the dark angel. The dark angel's knees were shaking. The sword stabbed into the darkness and the angel vanished away. The boy who was sitting there, eyes closed, now opened his eyes and hugged Charles. Beside the young camper's head appeared a new angel—white, lovely, handsome, and strong.

"Whoa!" William said aloud in complete amazement.

"What'd ya say?" Hector asked from the lower bunk. William peered over the side of his bunk, making sure to not be overheard.

"I just saw that kid's dark angel get killed, and a white angel appeared in its place," William said, astonished.

"You still on that dark and light angel stuff? You need to just relax, man . . . because you're starting to weird me out." Hector didn't look up from his sports magazine as he made his statement. William, disappointed in the lack of support from his best friend, lay on his back, staring at the ceiling. His dark angel, resting with his feet propped on his pillow, never seemed to close his eyes. William closed his eyes just as the lights to the cabin clicked off.

Charles shouted the poem for the night: *"Hazelnutters sleep well, and bath better because you smell, don't give me excuse of you being male, for its better if girls don't wail, so use the soap until it suds, and all will be swell! GOOD NIGHT!!"* The room filled with whispers and snoring and, of course, the occasional—and yet somehow rather regular—passing of wind. William lay paralyzed by the sight he had witnessed and desperately wanted to understand what it meant. William would pray that night right there in the darkness of the wooden-planked cabin—all to himself.

"Give me a white angel . . . please."

Feeling more contentment over this prayer, he fell asleep.

## CHAPTER THIRTY-ONE

# Saturday

The next morning, William's fuzzy feelings came to an explosive end as he found his mirrored reflection greeted once more by the proud, smiling dark angel behind his shoulders. William still did not understand that God is not a genie who can be told what to do; God's will is supreme.

At canteen breakfast, William sat with food in front of him and no appetite at all. William poked at his cinnamon oatmeal, hand tucked under his solemnly slouched face, carrying a weight too heavy to sit up straight. He was confused, frustrated, and most of all, sad. *What is wrong with me?* William was yelling inside. "Why can't I have a light angel?" he said out loud this time, but under his breath.

"Hi, William." William sat up straight now and turned his head to the familiar, yet gracefully sweet, voice of Penny.

"Um, hi, Penny." William was unable to hide his nervousness.

"Is this seat saved?" Penny gestured toward the open spot near him.

"It was Hector's seat, but you snooze, you lose. So the seat is all yours." Penny raises her eyebrows at the quick humor.

"No longer shaken up by the bobcat adventure, I see," Penny said with a smile, attempting to strike up a conversation.

"Yeah," William said causally, although he struggled to release the sadness that had trapped his thoughts. "I got to admit it; I was not expecting all of that. Were you?"

"Well, of course I did. I know people who know people," Penny said with her chin down, attempting her best mafia voice. They both laughed, recalling the creepy bobcat call and attempting it themselves—but poorly.

"So how are you, William?" Penny said with more intention now directed to the conversation.

"I'm fine," William answered.

"That's it? Just fine?" Penny asked, trying to get William to talk more.

"Yeah. How are you?" William asked, trying to get the attention off of him, and to stop saying "yeah" for all his conversation-starters—it was annoying to him, so surely it was annoying to everyone else.

"Asked you first," Penny quickly replied.

William's lips hung open as he was about to share more words, but then found he was speechless as he gazed above Penny for the first time since she sat down. The darkness that had hung as a halo above her was gone!

In its place, a glowing angel of light stood effortlessly, holding two curved Arabian blades! William's face lost all color. Not that he would be able to tell the difference in color with his vision still absorbing only shades of gray. His mind raced with confusion once again; he was unable to speak clearly.

"William, what's wrong?" Penny asked, seeing his jaw dropping low. William turned his head toward his food, now cold and dried out. Penny sensed that something big was on William's mind, for his eyes were fighting to hold in tears. "William, what is it?" She cared; she placed her warm hand on his arm.

A new voice suddenly filled William's ears: deep, rich, and eloquent: *"It is OK, William. Today is a good day. The light will soon hold you close."*

William moved his arm away, sending an unintentionally, non-friendly gesture. The voice was lovely and Penny was friendly; why did he pull away from the comfort of her friendship? The darkness behind him was marching in place, making a noisy ruckus, to keep William's emotions edgy. Penny pulled back even more, feelings hurt from William's response. She looked out toward the wall. "If you want to be alone . . ." Penny began to say, but was then interrupted by William.

"No! No!" William spoke quickly, not wanting her to leave. William was happy with Penny around, and couldn't find the words to share the unusual circumstance he found himself in.

"Then what is wrong?" Penny asked again, with much concern for her friend.

William closed his eyes, fighting with his thoughts of how to tell her, or wondering if saying anything would just scare her away. How was he to explain his undesired ability to see angels and demons? Yet he truly felt that it would be OK to chance this element of fear in order to gain more clarity on his predicament. He wanted to be able to see, but he was unable to comprehend. William took too long to respond, and so Penny spoke up.

"Well fine, if you're not going to tell me how you are, then I will tell you how I am."

William was not sure if she was mad at him or just needed to share her feelings. She continued: "Do you remember when we were at Hector's house?" William shook his head to say yes. "And do you remember when you asked me if I thought if I was pretty?" Penny asked, staring into William's eyes. William nodded his head "yes" again; he was completely mesmerized by Penny's new boldness. "But I didn't answer you then, and then you said you thought I was pretty."

William, lost for words, shook his head for "yes" once again, not knowing where this conversation was heading. Penny inhaled strongly, then spoke in her exhale: "Well . . . I am." The confidence came through strongly in Penny's voice. "I mean, I now know I am pretty. I didn't think I was pretty. When you asked me, I felt embarrassed because of the way I viewed myself. I kept thinking for days of the question you asked. What I am trying to say is . . . thank you." Penny was sincere and innocent in her statement.

William, entirely confused at the female mind and the timing in which all of this was happening, replied, "You're welcome." William did not know if this was the "more-than-friends" conversation that he always hoped for, but felt compelled to learn more about Penny's heart.

"How did you? . . . well, how did you come to know that you are pretty?" William said in a choppy mess of a sentence.

Penny answered by rephrasing William's attempt at a question. "You mean, what changed my mind?"

"Yeah, that's what I was trying to say," William said. "You don't have to share if you don't want to, if it's more girl talk-fitting or something like that."

"No, it's OK. I want to tell you." Penny was eager to say more.

"My camp counselor told me that I am created in the image of God, and that my beauty and confidence comes from God alone, and not from men. She explained that true beauty can't be bought at a store or painted on with makeup, but rather discovered when you use the mirror that God has provided. It was confusing at first, but once we talked about my family more, it clicked. I rarely hear from my dad that I am pretty, and when he does say it, it's only because of being super-dressed up for a special event. So when you said it to me that day, it was hard for me to hear it . . . rather, even more hard for me to believe it. I have a new perspective now; I feel pretty and I know I am because it's beauty of the heart, not skin, that matters."

"Wow! She said all that to you?" William said as a plan formulated on how to get a white angel of his own.

"No," Penny responded, not taking offense at William's short reply. "She said a lot more."

"Like?" William asked, with his hopes of knowing how his dark angel could be lifted.

"Like . . . beauty in God's image, salvation in Jesus, and living life for God, obeying Him and loving everyone . . . even enemies." Penny shared—and clearly so—all she had verbally downloaded from the previous night's conversation with her counselor.

"Wow, that's a lot of stuff." William was trying to process all he had just heard. "So you don't need your dad to call you pretty to feel pretty?" William asked, seeking more clarity.

"No, it's more than just a feeling of 'pretty,'" Penny said, wanting William to understand as she did. "It's . . . my counselor said . . . about believing in Jesus to forgive you for your wrong, not just the wrong you have done, you are doing, but that Jesus will even forgive what you will later do. She said that I can't do good to get to Heaven, but that only Jesus is good enough to allow me to have a friendship with God." Penny was glowing as she shared.

She reached into her pocket and retrieved a small piece of paper with some handwriting on it. "She wrote this verse down for me to remember. I want to read it to you." Penny looked directly at William.

"Yes," William quickly said, entranced at this newfound confidence that Penny held.

"John 3:16: For God so loved the world, that he sent His one and only Son, that whoever should believe in Him, will not die, but have life everlasting," Penny said. She looked up and smiled big.

"And you now believe all this?" asked William.

"With all my heart," Penny said convincingly.

"You gonna' eat that?" Penny said, pointing down to an untouched biscuit on William's plate. William picked it up to offer it to her, surprised at the transition of the conversation.

"Yep, I really like bread, all shapes and sizes," Penny said, taking the biscuit. She took a big bite, stuffed the bread to one side of her mouth, and said, "So William, do you think you're . . . man-pretty?"

William laughed and shook his head side to side. "No, I am man-gorgeous." They both laughed, but William knew the real answer was not so funny. Penny and William walked their trays to the kitchen window.

"I wonder where Hector is. He never misses breakfast," William said as they headed out of the canteen. They could hear the laughter of a large group steadily increasing as they opened the doors to the outside.

To their surprise, Hector was tied to the flagpole with a pair of dingy white underwear on his head. The counselors had been in a meeting and gave just enough time for the sneaky boys of cabin "Chest Hair" to take the unsuspecting Hector hostage and "panty-fy" his head. William, laughing along with the mob of kids surrounding this epic scene, ran to the aid of his friend. Although William had not been there to prevent the face wedgie, he was here now to rescue Hector from total and complete image destruction. William quickly gave sight to his blindfolded friend and freed his hands from the warm metal flagpole.

The eerie voice of darkness crept in his ears yet another time. *"A friend you are, this way of shared life, don't break the bond."*

William had lost his fear of hearing these angels and was instead becoming more and more frustrated at hearing their lies. Hector, the king of cool, stepped forward and took a grand bow for the crowd, as if he had performed some kind of magic trick. Unfortunately, though, no one clapped until the boys of Cabin 6 ran out of hiding to spank both Hector and William on the rumps as they ran away. The crowd hooped and hollered with approval. William and Hector decided to hurry back to their cabin to avoid more embarrassment and to not tattle-tell to the counselors about the hazing they had faced.

From there, the morning transitioned to craft time by the lake. They made friendship bracelets with beads on yarn string to the tune of upbeat music playing nearby. All the boys and girls were happy in the moment, soaking up the sunshine, making small talk with one another. It was the last day of camp and only one more night fire would be set ablaze. For all the times William had been to summer camp, he had never felt as much fear and anxiousness over songs and marshmallows as he did now. The water was calm, with small ripples forming at the feet of the cattails at the bank's edge. The sun glared into his eyes, but he didn't mind.

William found a heart bead and secretly snuck it onto his man-bracelet, followed by the letter P. He tried sorting the beads by shades of gray and found the lighter gray to be a bit more soothing and he hoped they were light blue.

"Dude, what's up with all the pink beads; you trying to tell me something?" Hector called out to William.

"Starting a new fad. Duh!" smooth William lied. In reality, it was the ultimate chick jewelry. The other side of the bracelet held the letters "BBB," which to Hector and William stood for "best buddies boo-ya." William proudly tied his stringed masterpiece to his wrist. In triumph, the two boys punched the sky with fists, revealing their "power," as if superheroes about to fly off to fight evil. Penny and her cabin of friends were sitting close by watching these two teens act like little boys.

After crafts, a canoe trip made for the last voyage around Gator Tear Lake. The boys always enjoyed attempting to sabotage one another on the canoes. Tipping a canoe was the ultimate prize on the lake. Hector and William tag-teamed an unsuspecting boat of "Chest Hair" campers, revenge for the underwear incident. The freshly painted shiny canoe tipped easily enough, sending the two campers into the water. In William and Hector's "victory dance" (inside their canoe) of tipping the other canoe, they themselves got proud and took a plunge into the murky water. But falling in was a great way to laugh and workout as they huffed and puffed to pull themselves over the side of water-filled canoe. Both dark angels belonging to William and Hector sat on the seats in the boat, awaiting their slow arrival. William's angel was carving a hole in the bottom of the boat; Hector's angel was holding out an arm and waving an imaginary scarf. This demon kept flicking his tongue, like some serpent. *Lovely face,* William thought before being startled by Hector's terrified scream. Hector pointed in the direction behind William, a great look of fear on his face.

William turned around to see a cotton mouth snake coming with speed and purpose to claim a victim for disturbing its nest. William panicked and tried getting in the boat with even more speed to avoid a life-threatening condition. Hector made it into the boat and raised an oar to swat the snake, which had paused to raise its head, ready to strike. The darkness bumped into Hector, causing him to lose his balance and control of the oar at the same time, sending it uselessly to the water below. "Help!" was all the struggling teen could say. Meanwhile, William closed his eyes and gripped the edge of the boat . . . awaiting the teeth to sink in and expecting a sharp, burning heat to find his exposed neck.

*Whomp!!* Another oar suddenly whacked the head of the serpent, followed by several more: *Whomp! Whomp! Whomp!* "Take that you creepy, nasty demon snake!" Penny held a triumphant smile and she swung the oar proudly at her side as a blade in a battle.

"Thanks. You saved my life," William said, still floating, with his life jacket bunched up to his throat.

"Well, I can't save lives, but I am training to be a lifeguard. Only Jesus can save lives . . . remember that," Penny said.

William's unwanted guardian was trying to throw his short blades into the heart of Penny, but before the blades would appear to hit their mark, the angel of light gracing her presence would block each attempt—with little effort. The dark angel appeared to have great strength . . . but Penny was protected. She was sealed with light that darkness could not penetrate.

"Well, see you for the fire time . . . no more snake hunting for you boys," said Penny in her best mom's voice.

"OK, OK," said William. "I can't make any promises though, ladies. I might need your help in the future." Here came the over-flirting Hector, and the girls ignored him completely. William stayed alongside the canoe and helped kick to get the boat back to the dock. William felt a tugging on his heart, a desire for relief building up inside his ribs, just waiting to be set free. But how?

The day was cooling down and dinner canteen was on its way. The meal would be all things fireside . . . hot dogs, chili dogs, marshmallows, and other processed foods kids love to eat and parents try to avoid. William found himself checking mirrors more than a girl does, hoping to see a new friend above his head—but the haunting darkness remained still. The sun continued to set; meanwhile, William found himself wanting to know more about the angel-transformation that had taken place with Penny. He wrote a note—more chicken scratching than letters—asking Penny to meet him at the dock 15 minutes before bonfire. The note was signed with a heart and his sloppy signature, followed by a P.S. statement: "Come alone . . . please."

William paced back and forth, awaiting his unclaimed lady, who he liked way more than a friend—though he was too scared to admit this. Penny came a minute earlier than he had asked, and this made William glad. She walked up, flashlight shining into his eyes and then down to his feet. "Oops, sorry, didn't see you there," Penny said, clumsily.

William held his hand up to block the light, and then smiled at her cute demeanor. "Nah, it's OK, Penny." Oh, how William loved to say her name.

"So what is this sneaky-message meeting all about?" Penny said in a whisper.

"Honestly, I want to ask you . . . umm . . . what's your relationship like with your dad?" William asked.

"What do you mean? . . . It's fine . . . well, I guess? . . . " Penny said, sounding confused.

William went on, attempting to explain. "Well, I mean, for me and my dad, we get along fine, but he doesn't really live the life he speaks of, like my grandpa did." Penny's face was confused. William did his best to clarify.

"My dad knows of God, but he doesn't do much about it," William said. "He seems to be a talk-the-talk but can't walk-the-walk."

"I know what you mean. I get along OK with my dad too, but until a few days ago, I looked to him for my self-esteem building, to hear that I was pretty in his eyes. But what I have come to realize is that man makes mistakes and will never be perfect, so why expect him to? I know now that Jesus, who was not man, but choose to be, is perfect and forever will be. I can put my hope and trust in Him, because He is never failing. Flawless; not like my earthly father, but always loving, finding me fearfully and wonderfully made." Penny could have shouted her words; she felt such passion in her heart for what she believed.

William listened intently to her heart being poured out. Penny let out a soft sigh of contentment; her face glowed with true joy. William wanted that joy so much. He couldn't contain his arms as they impulsively lifted up like zombie arms and pulled fragile Penny into an embrace. Penny couldn't react in time, but instead she was hoisted into the air, her arms being crushed to her sides. She attempted to pat William's back with one immobile hand. The lovely voice of light embraced him back, saying: *"God will set you free, you will have this peace, you will have true joy."* Just as quickly as William had attacked-hugged Penny, he let her go.

With a quick grab of both her shoulders in his hands, he blurted out, "Thank you!" and turned and ran away. Bewildered Penny remained still, eyebrows in confusion, and finally responded with "You're welcome."

William shouted, his voice trailing behind, as he continued to run toward the trees: "See you at the bonfire!"

William's feet were moving fast; instinctively, he knew what he had to do. He came up to Hector, out of breath; Hector already had two hot dogs toasting on the fire. "What took you so long, and what's up with your frozen smiley face?" Hector asked, focused more on the toasting of his mixed-meat meal than on William.

"Aww, I just got lost in the woods again," William said sarcastically.

"Yeah; well, while you've been off playing in the woods, I have been here all alone, cooking you a dog! So in advance, you're welcome," Hector replied, attempting a serious tone, but failing miserably.

"Oh, how kind of you," William said, mimicking his best girlie impression.

"Yeah, yeah. I know I am the best friend you could ever have," Hector shot back.

William felt sadness: with their creepy angels being of one cloth, what would happen to their friendship if he received an angel of light? William couldn't ponder the question any longer, because Charles stepped up onto one of the many benches by the fire and announced: "Tonight is the final night of camp. As we all know, it's a tradition that one member of each cabin share a tale from this week, so decide now who will be speaking. Keep it clean and keep it creative."

The stories lasted deep into the evening with much laughter and moments of happy tears. The jokes began to die down as the fire cooled to red, then white, then gray-white coals. Soon resembling an airplane's view of a city twinkling at night, the flames faded into ashes.

The fire no longer blazed as Ranger Howard stood to announce the final day's itinerary. "Attention campers! Just as a reminder to those of you who will be getting baptized at the lake tomorrow morning before canteen, meet at the dock at 6 a.m. If you are coming, be sure to tell your counselor."

Some logs were added to rekindle the flames for the final song of the evening. The campers linked arm in arm and swayed to the lyrics of the song, united in friendship, and some in faith. The song continued to rise up from around the golden glow of the fire, lighting the smiling faces and warming the hearts of the campers.

William slipped away from the crowd to quiet his thoughts and pray. William thought back to the prayer he had made a week ago and how different his life had become. The shadows of the trees hid his small, kneeling frame. William closed his eyes and talked with God.

"You are real God. You are perfect. . . . I am not. . . . But, of course you already know that. Sorry for my lies, for not choosing to do what is right. I want to be man-gorgeous, not with this dark, evil angel floating above my head. I see differently now. You are the Truth who will set me free. You are the giver of real joy. I am sorry I do wrong. Thank you that you love me . . . well, that you love everyone. . . . That you gave your Son to take my sin away. That although He had to die, He also came back to life, and I have the hope of knowing He will one day return again. It's still a bit confusing, but I want to know you more. Please give me a life of light. I know you're the only one who can. AMEN." The evil lurking shadow began to silently scream as his knees began quaking, and his face showing immense pain before vanishing into a blinding array of sunlight.

## CHAPTER THIRTY-TWO

# Renew You

William opened his eyes into the night, looked at his hands, and stood up. He didn't feel any different. He stepped out of the shadows of the night toward the campfire's light. There before him rose colorful red-and-orange deep shades of heat from the flames. Colors were there, jumping into his eyes! William rubbed his hands over his surprised eyes. This was real. His vision was seeing as he once did, but his perspective on its beauty was forever altered. The campers continued in their songs and harmonious swaying, their movements mimicking the flames as they danced. William looked around at those near the fireside; only campers were before him, no dark or light angels hung above them. He was made new: his sight, his mind, and most transforming of all: his heart.

He ran to Charles: "I want to go to the lake tomorrow." William's smile was shining brightly.

"Really?" Charles said in between a song verse. "That's great news! We will walk there together in the morning." William, walking with a new spring in his step, linked in with the circle and placed his hand on Hector's shoulder. No extra voices entered his ears. William sang loudly, in joy and gladness, ignoring his inability to keep a pleasing melody.

After the music drifted away and the glow from the fire looked nearly gone, a camp counselor from Cabin Chest Hair announced, in a shout: "Midnight slip-and-slide at Turtle Hill!" Hoots and hollers were made by everyone around the bonfire. Turtle Hill had earned its name back in '93 when Ranger John Howard broke the slip-and-slide record for most creative crash. He tied a green inner tube to his back and sprinted twenty feet before launching himself airborne like a superhero, landing on his back and spinning all the way through the mud pit and into the lake. Kids from then on always called that descent area Turtle Hill.

Everyone ran back to their cabins to change into the dirtiest clothes they could find. This was not difficult for the boys, whose clothes, by the end of the camping week, had all developed a stink or severe stain to them. The girls, however, had a much more difficult time deciding. The girls discussed whether or not their gray shirt would match their brown shorts or what to do if mud got in their hair or how the slip-and-slide might mess up their makeup.

Back at Hazelnut Cabin #8, William and Hector were putting Charles's underwear on over their pants in an attempt to be extra spirited. Suddenly there came a knock at the door. All laughter halted immediately. One of the Hazelnutters opened the door, then slammed it and yelled to his fellow cabin mates: "IT'S A GIRL!" All the boys ran to the door with quick feet and even faster heart beats. The same Hazelnut camper cracked the door open, peeped his head outside, and whispered, "What's the password?"

"Come on, open the door," said the girl, standing outside.

"What is the password?" he demanded once more, this time in a much louder whisper.

"Just open the door! . . . " The girl spoke now with an annoyed tone.

"Password!" he said again.

"Fine. Boys rule and girls drool." The girl rolled her eyes at the immaturity of this cabin boy.

"Told you! Boys rule and girls drool!" the boy announced aloud. The Hazelnutters tribe broke out in a dance in a big circle, thinking they were so cool. The door opened wide enough for those inside to be fully seen.

"Dude," Hector said to William, elbowing his side to stop his dancing. "It's Penny."

William, frozen from his chanting, stood still and stared at Penny. William looked down at his attire, realizing Charles's underwear currently still resided on the outside of his pants. Unable to hide himself, he decided to simply wave. "Hey Penny," William said with a half-smile of embarrassment. Penny smiled at the sight of William, her cheeks blushing; she motioned with her eyes for him to come outside.

The cabin boys couldn't resist making "Oooooooo" and "Ahhhhhhh" sounds, acting as immature as teen boys are. Both Penny and William were blushing now.

Penny spoke first. "I wanted to know if I could wear one of your shirts for the slip-and-slide; mine are all packed."

"Then unpack them!" shouted a camper, listening in on the conversation.

William and Penny's faces continued to redden. William wanted to tell her all about his new sight and how he was certain he was now man-gorgeous, but the situation didn't seem to carry the right timing. The boys in the cabin continued taunting the pair with comments.

"Give her your shirt, Willy Billy!"

The pressure of the cabin boys and the distraction of Penny's smile pushed William to act first and think later. William reached over his neck to rip off his shirt in the manliest way possible, but his lack of practice, and lack of focus, turned his "muscle display" into a comedy routine. William looked like a dog trapped under a blanket rather than like one of the classy movie maneuvers he was envisioning. The cabin-ers cheered. William stood there red-faced and muscle-less, inhaling as much as he could handle to appear stronger. Finally, he got the shirt off and handed it to Penny.

"Thanks," she simply said and began to walk away.

"Actually," William said to Penny, causing her to turn around, "I wore that all day. It kinda' smells." He grabbed the same shirt he just had gifted to Penny and ran back inside the cabin. Penny's hand remained frozen in space from the item snatched from her hand. William soon ran back outside and filled her empty hand with a less-smelly shirt of his.

"Here . . . you can keep it," William said, smiling big and feeling victorious in helping Penny for a change.

"Thanks," Penny said again and walked away, turning back to smile at him once more before continuing on her way. All the boys of the cabin cheered again, adding whistles and claps to the mix. William put the same stinky shirt back on and headed to Turtle Hill.

The slip-and-slide was classic. Everyone got as soapy as possible before colliding full speed with the plastic tarp and wiggling and spinning downward into a massive mud pit. Covered with wet earth, the campers crawled or ran up the hill to do it all over again. At 1:30 a.m., Ranger Howard got on the microphone and announced, "Mud monsters, the slip-and-slide is now closed. Gather for a photo at the dock in two minutes. GO! GO! GO!" he shouted in his best military commander voice.

Everyone, whether freshly mudded or already drying, ran

out to the dock. Girl photo first, followed by the boys, and then a big group shot. The picture was snapped with smiles and random goofy faces, the one or two nose pickers, and those who linked their arms around each other to make the moments all the more memorable. Camp was becoming the best time of the summer instead of the worst.

Ranger Howard got onto the microphone again, this time telling the campers, "OK, party animals, time to clean up. Use outside showers first. Those meeting at the lake, be there at 6 a.m. Sleep well; you have a big day ahead of you. GOOD NIGHT, AND GOD BLESS!"

Sleeping was the furthest thing from William's mind; he was filled with more excitement than a child getting training wheels off their bike. Searching for God is not you finding Him, it's *God inviting you in*, William now realized. William's heart began searching for the difference in this truth. His eyes had become awakened to the world of spiritual warfare and its reality. He had come to see, outwardly, the saved and unsaved hearts through a living light or darkness guardian angel.

William had been given a great glimpse at the fates of those around him, bound to Heaven or bound for Hell. William knew now, without a shadow of doubt, that his hope of Heaven was real and that he would be there. He had seen a real fight of good against evil and knew that salvation was the only way to win. For no one will escape death; but a new life can be made in Christ, he now realized. William would not hide his new-found light; he would shine it as a beacon into the darkness. He had no fear, for he knew God was always there.

## CHAPTER THIRTY-THREE

# Explain It Plain

With the 'Nutters all cleaned up and avoiding sleep, they filled the morning hours with laughter and practical jokes. Although William felt great relief at having his vision back and joy beyond joy at finding the light, he felt unsure how he should approach those around him. How would he know who was saved? Charles shared a Bible verse, referring to faith without deeds being dead. William thought also how actions speak louder than words, and he decided that that's how he would know. William lay on the lower bunk, hands resting behind his head and staring at the signatures of campers of the past displayed on the gum-crusted plywood bunk above. He squinted his eyes to a name that seemed familiar . . . was it really a coincidence, or another perfectly orchestrated event in life? He read the name aloud. Edgar James Jones was scratched into the worn wooden frame. The name he read was . . . his dad's name. "Well, I'll be," William said to himself. William would come to understand all the more how different light and darkness could be, breaking some friendships and strengthening others. Despite the uproar of his hyperactive bunkmates, William fell asleep with little effort.

The sun came quicker than expected, and so did the alarm. William and Hector slept through the first chiming of the alarm clock, but Charles was already up. Charles did not delay in assisting the boys to wake up more promptly, using an all-encouraging pillow to provide a face-slam sandwich. Unfortunately for William, he lay there unable to defend himself. His arms that had once been so peacefully placed under his sleeping head were now past the stage of feeling like sand and instead felt more like absolute numbness. They were as helpful as a potato in a snow storm.

"Hurry up, William; this morning is the big splash. You don't want to be late!" Charles whispered so he would not disturb the other campers. William used his functioning legs as leverage to get his body over the bunk. Thankfully, he was on the bottom bunk this time, or he would have had major issues getting down from the top with his rubber arms. William stood tall, feet finding the cool wooden floor and his arms slumped at his side. He didn't have time to change or the ability to lift his arms. He turned to leave. He would have to wear what he slept in to the baptism. His hands were uselessly trailing behind him like a swan dive gone haywire. William stared down at his wardrobe choice of swishy running shorts, a bit too short to be cool, and a gray T-shirt stained with some form of chocolate . . . he hoped, at least, that was chocolate.

He looked more like a first-grader at a slumber party than a teenager about to be baptized.

"Come on, man! Clock is ticking! We have to be there at the dock in three minutes. Hope those shorts are ready for some jogging," Charles said, clapping his hands to encourage speediness. William ran behind Charles, his hands slapping his sides out of rhythm all the way to the lake.

The meeting was already in session when William and Charles arrived. Ranger Howard was addressing the 30-person crowd. Each cabin was represented. Ranger Howard, strong and clear and not needing a microphone to amplify his speech, allowed the water to work as his most powerful form of acoustics.

"For those that have come this morning to be baptized, I commend your faith. You should know that baptism is not a requirement to be saved or a prerequisite to go to Heaven. Baptism is simply an outward expression of an inward faith. You will be declaring to the public the God you believe in and the life you will live. Each camper will be baptized by their cabin leader. Please break up into groups for the next 15 minutes and talk with your counselor about what steps you can make to be a true Jesus follower after being baptized. Congratulations and live your testimony in mind, body, and spirit."

With that, Ranger Howard ended his announcement and allowed the groups to split up and spread out on the grassy hillside. William was the only Hazelnutter in attendance to be baptized this morning. Charles said to William, "Do you understand all that Ranger Howard said about baptism?"

"Yeah, I understand it," William responded.

"So, what about the angel story you shared with me in the backyard before camp? You still being haunted by a dark shadow?" Charles asked, concerned that William didn't truly understand salvation.

William sat more straight than ever with the confidence he now held. "Well, when we nearly died by that near-bus crash, I started to wake up to the thoughts of, if I did die, where would I go? ... I didn't feel confident.... I didn't think "hell." Of course, no one does; but I didn't feel sure about Heaven either. I do know now. I have the Jesus ticket and I am on the list to go when it's my time to be called back home."

"That is an amazing story. What a life to live, and to see the truth of spiritual warfare and receive the light. Welcome to the club! Let's pray," Charles added.

"Umm, sure. I'll go first," William said, beginning his prayer. "God, thank you for letting me go to camp this summer and for everyone in my life. Thank you for saving me through your Son Jesus. I ask that my baptism would let people know what I believe in and that I would live out my testimony as Ranger Howard said. I pray that my dad would be saved and that Hector would be saved. Amen."

"Amen, that was an awesome prayer. I am so glad you are friends with my brother; hopefully your new faith will rub off his darkness," Charles said, thinking of the great potential of having a best-friend influence on his brother.

"William!" A voice called from a distance. William looked around to see who was calling his name. "Hey William, over here!" his dad called out. His mother was lifting a tissue to her eyes as she waved with her free hand. Was she crying? Why do moms always cry, even when they're happy? William waved back and walked over to them, surprised at seeing them here at camp so early.

He hugged his parents and asked, "What are you doing here so early? Pickup is not until lunch." William was both glad and confused that they were there.

"We came to see you get baptized," his mom said, pulling her son into another embrace.

"How did you know I was getting baptized?" asked William, his mom having let go of the boa constrictor mom-hug.

"We got a call late, late last night from Charles," his dad said, motioning with his head toward Charles, who still sat on the grass nearby.

"Your dad and I are very proud of you, William," his mom said, trying her best to not allow her eyes to leak out happy, salty tears again.

William noticed Penny from his peripheral vision and then interrupted an almost-sobbing moment from his mom.

"I am going to go say hi to someone. I will be right back," William said, turning to leave. William ran to Penny to greet her with a morning hello.

"Who is that?" William's dad asked aloud to Charles, who had strolled his way over to the parents to say hello.

"Oh, that's Penny. They're good friends," Charles said with a casual tone.

William's father felt like he was watching his son growing up before his eyes as he talked with the young girl before him.

"Good morning, Penny," William said, wanting to hug her, but refraining.

"Good morning, William," Penny responded with freshness in her voice and attention in her eyes.

"I am getting baptized," William said, quickly.

"Really? Me too!" Penny responded with excitement. Knowing full well that only those meeting at 6:00 am would of course be getting baptized, but she was excited to see him there so she swallowed the sarcastic remark and voiced a factual one. "I saw you with your parents over there," Penny said, motioning to where they were standing.

William turned toward his parents and then back to her and said. "Yeah, surprised me. I didn't know they were coming. . . . Where is your dad?"

Penny smiled softly, sadness in her eyes, expressing that he would not be coming; she didn't need words to give this message to William. William, realizing Penny was troubled, decided to use humor to bring her comfort.

"I'm sorry, Penny. . . . Would you want to wear my shirt again?" He reached up as if to take off his shirt again. Penny broke into laughter and grabbed the bottom of his shirt, tugging on it to make sure it would remain.

"No, no—please keep it on. Gray is not my color, anyways." William felt proud that he had turned her frown upside down. "William," Penny said, pausing and choosing sincere words. "You're ... man-gorgeous."

William smiled from ear to ear, nodded, and put back on his serious face, replying, "Thanks Penny. You're lady-pretty."

Penny now smiled brightly. "Thank you."

Penny had grown fond of William's gentleness, and William found Penny to be more than wonderful.

# CHAPTER THIRTY-FOUR

# All Said and Done

The image of his son rising up out of the water froze in William's father's mind . . . and softened his heart. William, still wet and smelling like a fish, walked to his dad, hugged him, and in the confidence of a whisper, "I have a light angel."

William's dad gave a blank stare to his son. "You saw it turn white?" William's father responded.

"No . . . I don't see anyone's angels anymore. Well, since I become saved and all."

His dad stood still, not knowing what to say or to do next. William understood by his father's demeanor that he was processing a bit too much information. William hoped that one day his father would come to understand it all fully.

William's mom walked up to the two of them and asked, "William, you want to show us where breakfast is?"

"Follow me, please, to Canteen . . . or as we like to say, 'SEE FOOD.'" William led the way as he dripped dry as they followed the other campers to eat. "I am going to run and change and I will meet you up there," William said as he directed his parents to continue up the hill to the building marked "CANTEEN."

"OK, sunny boy," his father said as he wrestled with his own internal darkness. William sprinted—partially skipped—from the joy he felt. William arrived at his cabin, whipped open the door, chin held high and chest up and raised, expecting a round of applause from all the Hazelnutters, but instead was greeted by Hector alone. All the other boys were busy getting packed and dressed for the last morning's events.

"Yo, how was swimming with the fishes?" Hector said while tying his shoe.

"It was great. Penny was there, and both my parents came," William shared with excitement.

All the campers had to have their things packed up and placed on the front porch of their cabins before breakfast. William was quick and orderly, getting his soggy drawers switched for dry ones.

"Hey, hurry up!" William called to Hector.

"Me, hurry up? I am not the one daintily rolling my boxers into origami," Hector replied.

"It's a way to save space, thank you very much," William said, continuing his folding.

The breakfast bell rang in the distance, loud enough to be heard by any hungry camper miles away. The boys stuffed the rest of their items into the bags provided for them and threw them onto the porch; their bodies darted to Canteen like bugs to a light bulb. William could see his parents standing together, watching the campers crowding the doors. Breakfast for today was all the leftovers from the week, a little of this and a little of that, mixed with the not-sure-what- that-is category.

The morning meal transitioned quickly as each camper easily stepped into the role of tour guide, leading parents and siblings around the camp they had called home for the past week. Hector walked beside William and William's parents and added in his own memories made. William's dad followed his joyful son with much interest and excitement, but couldn't wrap his thoughts around how, in just a week's time, his son's heart had transformed from dark to light.

The boys would high-five fellow "Nutters" as they walked about, or give the fist-to-forehead secret cabin sign as they passed by. The final stop on the tour was the bonfire circle. William walked to and then sat on the bench where he had prayed only the evening before.

"This is where it all changed," William said, his eyes staring at the bench as he petted the wood grain.

"What change?" said Hector, the first to say what both parents were wondering.

"Where I became saved," William said in a matter-of-fact tone.

"Oh, and this is where Hector nearly set his shoe on fire from a flaming marshmallow," William blurted out. Quickly jumping to his feet as he recalled another memory by the fire, he left the bench behind him.

William's father looked down at the bench and then up at his son, who was now rambling on about something . . . "Charles, something . . . something . . . Cougar . . . something . . . a flashlight" . . . the rest of the words vanished into the sun that was reflecting off of Gator Tear Lake. The three of them continued to walk ahead, leaving a distressed father to his own thoughts.

William was sitting on a kayak, driving it like a car, and Hector using an oar as a cannon, while William's mom laughed nearby. William's father sat down on the bench where his son had just been and closed his eyes, breathing heavily from the load of emotion on his chest.

"Come on, Dad, no time for sitting!" William hollered.

But there was a strong war raging on inside his father. William's dad stood up, but the heavy burden of darkness brought him to his knees. In this moment, William's father fought his heart and wouldn't allow it to submit to the greatness of God. In his pride he stood up, unable to humble himself and to give up control and allow God to fully lead.

His heart ached, but he pushed it all aside.

## CHAPTER THIRTY-FIVE

# Fairwells

The four joined up again and traveled back to William and Hector's cabin. All the stuff was on the porch, but William rushed inside to grab his journal from the safety of an old mattress. William threw his pillow and journal into his dad's hands. "Can you hold this?" William asked, without waiting for a response.

"You brought it with you?" William's father said, a smile on his face as he held the tattered spine.

"Yeah, I tried to write something about the day's events, each night," William said, picking the crusted mud formed on the laces of his boots.

"Ready to go?" asked William's mom, holding her purse with both hands in front of her. Hector and William said their farewells with a man-hug and arm punch. Charles would be taking

Hector home, so it would be just William and his parents to converse on the drive home.

William trudgingly carried his stuff to his parents' car. Not the sportiest of vehicles, but it did what it was designed to do, most of the time. His dad opened the trunk and then got into the passenger side, allowing his wife to do the driving. William was reaching far into the trunk, rustling with his bags and shoes, attempting to organize his mess.

"William . . . is that you?" A voice soft and sweet floated into the cramped space. Startled, William tried to stand, but failed to avoid the roof of the trunk on his way up. William turned, hand rubbing his bruising skull. But his pain didn't seem to exist when he saw Penny standing there, in a blue sky cotton sundress, her hair untamed and laying to one side. He thought his heart might stop.

"Uhh . . . ouch! . . . You alright?" Penny said with a wince, knowing William's head must be throbbing.

"No, no, I was just testing the durability of the trunk with my head," William said, tapping the trunk's side with his fist. "Not my favorite activity, but someone's got to do it." Williams continued trying a bit too hard to be cool. He let out the air he had been holding in his chest to make himself look stronger, and exhaled, leaving a frail boy.

"So, I wanted to give you a hug, and this . . . scarf . . . handkerchief-y thing," Penny shyly stated, holding out her hand straight, with a blue-flowered cloth floating in the wind.

"Really, for me? Wow, thanks. I never had a 'hand scarf' before," William said in genuine appreciation.

"Handkerchief," Penny replied, politely correcting him.

"Right, handkerchief. And what about this hug? . . . " William said, smoothly reaching for a hug as he finished the sentence.

This time it was a proper hug, with both hands around her back and each resting their chin on the other's shoulder. It was picture-worthy, although they would not need a camera to re-

HICCUP EFFECT

member this moment. The parents sat quietly, watching their son play Mr. Cool from the convenience of their rearview mirror.

"I will see you soon, Penny," William said as he closed the trunk without looking.

"Yeah, see you soon." Penny stood there repetitively twirling her hair, standing sweetly in her hand sown fashion designed from a worn out button up shirt that was her dads. So crafty, that Penny

"Penny?" William said with a pause. When she turned to him, William softly said: "You're beautiful." William was fully locked on her deep, penetrating eyes. Penny smiled big and nodded her head thanks, too pleased to respond in words.

William got in the car and looked back several times at Penny before finally closing the door. Both parents quietly looked at one another as he entered the vehicle.

"Ready to go?" William's dad spoke, pretending it had not taken so long to place his things in the trunk. The car bumped and rocked along the gravel road. The trees were thick and they shaded the small metal car as it left Happy Howard Ranch. William, with full peace in his heart, closed his eyes and drifted to sleep.

It was comfortable with the chilled air pumping through the vents, a pleasant escape from the humid summer air outside. . . .

. . . A hiccup squeaked from William's lips.

William's eyes opened from the surprise hiccup to find the roof of the compact car was now a canvas ceiling. He lay still, scanning from left to right. He was back to the night this all began, the night he was struck by lightning at Blue Hill Forest. William paralyzed to move from his sleeping bag sat up, unable to comprehend his predicament. *You have got to be kidding me . . . seriously, you have got to be kidding me, he said to himself.*

A worn-out horn beeping a tone of a high-to-low struggling melody pulled William back to the present moment. William quickly looked to the road to discover Charles's classic green and white open-bed pickup truck wobbling up the gravel road, just as it had before what seemed years ago.

"Hey there, little man, come to bring you home after your big adventure in the woods," Charles called out from the open window.

"No way. . . . No way," William said, feeling dizzy with confusion. "How could I be in Blue Hill campground this second, when I just was at Happy Howard Ranch? How hard was I struck by lightning?" William rubbed his head, checking to make sure no lightning bolt scar was on his head. He looked down and saw a turtle, this time it was not struggling on his back, but rather walking slow and steadily away from his tent. *What is going on here?* Thought William, whose heart, it seemed, was collapsing in on its self. *Could a teen have a heart attack?* William hoped not.

"Nice to see you, too. Awesome bed hair, by the way," Charles said, chuckling as he opened the door. There was no angel haloing Charles head.

William's campsite was haphazardly thrown into the back of Charles's truck bed, bear- hugging the tent, with all contents still inside, to speed up the process.

"Easy there bud, what's the rush?" Charles said.

Grabbing the door and stepping inside with great eagerness to leave, William told Charles, "I need you to drive me to Penny's house."

"Wow, when did you get so bold, and who is Penny?"

"God revealed more truth to me than I could have dreamed," William said, rubbing his knees to come to grips with it all being just a dream. . . or had this been his future of what would be to come?

"You look determined. You on some kind of mission or something?" Charles asked.

"She needs to know her heart doesn't have to stay empty,"

William said, focused on the road ahead.

"Well alright, then. Let's go make dreams come true," Charles said, switching the stick shift to a higher speed.

"You have no idea. After last night, my entire perspective has been flipped upside down," William said. "Dreams never felt so real—or my reality so full of purpose. Last night I went to bed empty, this morning I awoke renewed. My heart is in Christ and is full of light, I can't hide it, I have got to shine it . . ."

The truck slowed, to a house with future conversations yet to be had by two boys and a girl by a windows light. William stepped eager to meet his dreams delight and praying truth would be shared and received with love instead of freight of all that he knew from one night.

Delighted, with nerves quivering in his throat, William inhaled strongly and reached his fist toward the faded, splinter-friendly door, ready to give a knock. His hand nearly pounded Penny in the nose as she hastily threw open the door. Penny stood tall, a smile dancing across her freckled cheeks. William inhaled strongly, once again, to begin his speech of how he would share his care for her, when she interrupted his exhale with a sentence that made William stagger: "An angel told me you would come."

**Faith will fill an empty heart.**

William now has grown into a man at the age of fourteen, but speaks as if he is forty. William is hunched over a desk of worn wood scribbling notes down swiftly. An aquarium containing a painted turtle, the one William saw on the day of this *un* ordinary day sat on display beside him. It would be his daily reminder that even when you feel you can't get up and you're struggling to find your way. God is the only one that can flip you right side up and save the day.

Sometimes in our lives great challenges must happen to

change lives, other times a dream to give insight. But what I realized in that moment of seeing my dreams so real was that I can't be passive, but a man of action. It took triumphantly overcoming color blindness, facing fear, finding hidden beauty, and becoming a man, through salvation, for me to realize I was dead. My body was an empty shell posing as a believer and playing a part to fit in with the world. I called myself a Christian on the outside. It may have looked that way, but on the inside my heart was dark and lifeless.

"God awoke me from my slumber, reminding me of the passage in Psalm 13:9: 'The light of the righteous shines brightly, but the lamp of the wicked is snuffed out.' Reading my Bible on a regular basis will be my armor to fight this spiritual battle we call life, and sharing with all how to change a heart of darkness to light. My anxious thoughts of not fitting in had been a shadow over my friends, preventing them from growing. I was too scared to stand alone, but not anymore.

"I have the peace that surpasses all understanding and the true joy that makes me happy long-term, not based on my circumstances. God can reveal my future in a dream's delight or through any method he chooses. He created the world and he created my story to share.

God has called me to make it known to all, so I will turn my dream into a book . . . maybe calling it *The Hiccup Effect,* or something strange—and then see what else God uses for hearts to change."

# The End

**BECOMING APART OF THE WAR OF PEACE**

We have all been given knowledge
of good and evil in true light

The ability to accept and be saved by
grace through faith not sight

Understanding that there is an endless
war of wrong and right

And the choice to join Jesus Christ in
this battle to fight the good fight

# Epilogue

Seven years passed + two days + thirty three minutes + give or take nineteen seconds, after the time William walked to the door of his more than wonderful friend Penny, to tell her of his dream reality only to be confronted with her knowledge already given from by an Angel.

At the cottage of Penny Rose Copper.

Footsteps parade up the stairs towards a very familiar door. A nervous hand quivering as it reaches to take hold of a tiny black velvet box deep within his jean pockets. *Will she say yes?* Thoughts demanding his body to take action although he had not fully thought through the recourse of an answer of "no." Knuckles clenched tight white with fear of the unknown. He reached with quickness to knock on a door in hopes of being taken in welcoming arms.

A rhythm of drumming reached delicate unsuspecting ears. Penny checked the side window first to see who was knocking on her front door. *Could it be?* The unlocking sound was conformation of a knock well heard. The hinges rubbed and squeaked open, Penny elegant and calm gave her astonished greeting.

Hector?

**To be left in suspense...until book two**
**"beTween" release date January 2016**

# About the Author

Married for life, Josiah and Nicole Newmaster love God's book, The Bible. They have moved twelve times in five years, fully renovating homes and reselling them. It has brought about many gray hairs, but they can each say the stressful work has paid off. All glory goes to God; and they realize without God's blessing and provision through family and friends, they would not be where they are today. Josiah teaches English and Math at an alternative high school. He enjoys long-distance running and having deep, thought-provoking discussions. Nicole likes playing dress up and being creative through dance and art. Having two daughters alongside their many adventures makes the memories all the more sweet. Realizing that everyone can go through seasons of life feeling like an awkward turtle, with our own plans thrown upside down, Josiah and Nicole hope to paint a picture of how to best view the circumstances they have been given, knowing only God to set them right side up again. They want to help bridge the gap, both cross-culturally and locally to love the world as Jesus did.

Flip right in to the next story by J.N. Newmaster by visiting www.jnnewmaster.com